The Dentist Chair

Brooklynn Nicole

PAGE PUBLISHING, INC.
New York, NY

First originally published by Page Publishing, Inc. 2017

Proofreading: Jill Hardin, Ruthie M. Bufford

This novel is a fictional work of writing. Similarities to places, names of persons, or incidents are purely coincidental.

ISBN 978-1-63568-949-5 (Paperback)
ISBN 978-1-63568-950-1 (Digital)

Printed in the United States of America

Preface

Life is not black or white, nor is it determined by the assurance or expectation of perfection promised at birth, when parents proclaim to love you unconditionally and be there when you are sick, sad, hurt, angry, in trouble, or facing the realities of life. However, the colors of life are complicated. Finding the one you wear best is always difficult, and you will most certainly be tested by the trials and tribulations of everyday living.

As an author, I write to express myself and my feelings, and I hone my skills of creativity through my inherited right as a form of freedom of expression. In every work of fiction, there is an element of truth, no matter how insignificant it may appear. The mystery to the reader is discerning truth from fiction. Fact or fiction is, without a doubt, determined by life experiences and the color of the glasses through which life has revealed itself... only to you. What is your truth?

Montgomery Valley County Courthouse
The Verdict (August 15)

After four antagonizing, gruesome, and exhausting months, the trial of *Dr. Harry James Maddox v. Montgomery Valley* was over. It took the jury of seven men and five women two days to reach a verdict. Dr. Maddox sat through a very excruciating and embarrassing trial where he was dissected, criticized, dehumanized, and sickened by false testimonies. He had been tried, judged, and convicted prior to the beginning of the trial and felt speaking on his behalf was useless. Harry and Katrina arrived at the courthouse as a unified couple, but Katrina was struggling to remain his pillar of strength and support. The pressure of the trial and working full-time aged her significantly. His attorney greeted them with what he felt was great news. All evidence provided was insufficient to convict him of first-degree murder; however, the jury may have perceived his refusal to testify as an indication of guilt. They prayed that short of a miracle he would be found guilty of involuntary manslaughter, a charge carrying a sentence of one to four years in a federal prison. If indicted, his license to practice dentistry would be revoked.

The tension was thick inside the small and overcrowded courthouse. The wait, coupled with the anticipation of the verdict, had become more than Natasha could manage. Was it the smell of perspiration mixed with an assortment of colognes and perfumes that was making her sick, or was it guilt? She felt weak, and her head was spinning. Had she done the right thing? Could she have said anything that might have changed the outcome? Her best friend was dead. Dr. Harry James Maddox, once the most prominent dentist in the tristate area, had been reduced to the most despised. One thing for certain, nothing can bring Linda back. He made his bed; now let him wallow in it.

The residents of this upscale and intimate city sat anxiously awaiting the verdict. Each testimony, even at the risk of embarrassment and shame, had been so explicit and graphic that minors and cameras were banned. Newspaper articles were carefully censored to protect the sensitivity of this fragile community. Each patient was understandably concerned about her personal vulnerability but bound by duty and loyalty to protect her beloved community and was more than willing to give her perceived account to have her day in court. Their husbands, curious and equally fearful of hearing the details, chose not to be present. Montgomery Valley and its lily-white residents had been changed forever.

As a minor, Cheryl Davis was questioned in the judge's chamber without the presence of a jury. The prosecution wanted desperately to add the charge of statutory rape, but she did not remember anything unusual, nor had there been evidence of inappropriate behavior. Out of concern, her parents made an appointment to take her to an ob-gyn to ensure her virginity was intact; however, she saved them the embarrassment by confessing that she was in her third year of college and was no longer a virgin.

Dressed in a navy-blue Armani suit, a white tailored shirt, and a paisley tie, Harry remained the picture of perfection at six feet four inches tall and weighting two hundred and ten pounds. He sat cradling his face in the palm of his hands, reflecting over the past four years. The room rapidly closed in around him, almost smothering him. He wondered how life strayed so far from perfection to this living hell. He hated himself. At the reality of what he might hear, he stared at the floor, shaking his head in anger and disbelief. With balled fist, he hit his legs over and over asking, "Why… why… why?" The tears of remorse he tried so desperately to hold back began to fall to the floor.

At ten o'clock sharp, the jurors entered the courtroom, each avoiding direct eye contact with Harry or his attorney. Harry turned to Katrina, who was seated directly behind him, and she lowered her eyes to the floor. His heart, heavy and racing out of control, sank within his chest, and he was unable to focus because nothing was more important than her support. He wanted to scream out and beg for her forgiveness. He was looking for reassurance, but the part of Katrina that once loved him unconditionally wanted to shout out, "I see you, and I am here for you," but the conflicted person she had become was filled with hurt, anger, and mortification and wanted to become invisible. She questioned her sanity, trying to understand why she was still here, then remembering a portion of her vows that he had obviously forgotten, "For better or for worse, in sickness and in health, until death we do part," made it crystal clear.

Harry reached up to wipe away the tears as he heard the bailiff say, "All rise… The Honorable Judge Jacob Patterson presiding… You may be seated." As he sat down, he turned again to Katrina. This time she looked into his eyes. Without speaking and after what seemed like an eternity and feeling that he was choking on his own saliva, he turned back to face the judge.

Judge Patterson addressed the jury, "Have you reached a verdict?"

"We have, Your Honor," said the foreman.

Turning to Harry, the judge said, "Dr. Maddox, stand and face the jury of your peers." Then readdressing the jury, he asked, "What is the decision of the jury?"

"Your Honor, on count one, on the charge of first-degree murder, we, the jury, find the defendant, Dr. Harry James Maddox, not guilty. On count two, on the charge of statutory rape, we, the jury, find the defendant, Dr. Harry James Maddox, not guilty. On count three, on the charge of involuntary manslaughter, we, the jury, find the defendant, Dr. Harry James Maddox, guilty. On counts four through eleven, on eight counts of rape, we the jury find the defendant, Dr. Harry James Maddox, guilty." There was a quiet cheer echoing throughout the courtroom as Harry slumped uncontrollably down into his chair.

Addressing the jury, the judge asked, "I assume this to be the consensus of the jury?" He polled each juror, "Juror number 1, juror number 2…" until all jurors had been polled reaffirming their decision. Turning back to Harry, the judge said, "Please stand, Dr. Maddox."

His body had become dead weight as the bailiff struggled to get him to his feet. What he heard next surprised Harry and his attorney. "Dr. Maddox, I found this trial to be extremely disturbing. This court will reconvene in six weeks when I will announce sentencing. It is also the decision of this court to revoke bail, and you will be remanded to the county jail until sentencing. I consider you to be a flight risk. Your wife is hereby ordered to surrender your passport, birth certificate, and driver's license to your attorney within twenty-four hours, or she shall be held in contempt of court." Once again, addressing the jurors, he said, "Thank you for your service, and you are now dismissed."

In handcuffs and with tears streaming down his face, Harry was led toward the exit but stopped and turned to look for Katrina. She looked away, detesting the sight of him. Pretending to be the dutiful wife had become hard. Inwardly, she was happy the judge revoked bail. Full of shame, she wanted to run as far from Montgomery Valley as possible. She assumed each testimony was true because he never attempted to offer an explanation. She left it up to him to explain his actions, but now she was left to draw her own conclusion, guilty as charged. The last thing she heard before leaving the courthouse was Harry's muted voice screaming her name, but she refused to look in his direction.

Prologue

Montgomery Valley is snuggled deep in the basin of Southern California and is a proud and unique community founded over two hundred years ago. If there is a utopia, this is it. Seventy percent of its residents are decedents of its founding fathers and continue to own the majority of the local businesses. Each family has a place, knows and respects that place, and breaking through the invisible barrier is next to impossible. Becoming a fully accepted member of the community is not a right, but a privilege. Marriage to outsiders is extremely rare and socially forbidden. Few ever have the right blood, the proper education, or money old enough to become true Montgomerians, and those that do, well, it comes at a very high price.

When you mix the old with the new, it reacts much like oil and vinegar, combining temporarily but quickly returning to its natural state. The oil eventually rises to the top, and the vinegar remains on the bottom, bitter and pungent as ever. Even with sugar added, it maintains an air of bitterness.

Let me formally introduce you to Montgomery Valley's oil and vinegar.

Cheryl Davis (Oil)

Cheryl Davis was born and raised in Montgomery Valley with a silver spoon in her mouth and is the only child of Chauncey and Julie. Her claim to fame is being a spoiled-over pampered brat. At sixteen, Cheryl's major crime in life is vanity. She is the typical self-centered cheerleader who would kill to be at the top of the pyramid. She is beautiful in her own right and knows it. She has no difficulty letting anyone who crosses her path know that she knows it. She has plenty of friends, all of the same breeding and mind-set. It is amazing how well everyone gets alone without killing one another. When troubles arise, the parents of these spoiled monsters always manage to out purchase one another to soothe disenchanted waters. There is a Mediterranean cruise, a trip to the French Rivera, or some other expensive ploy dangling in front of the girls to appease the situation. Her parents come from old money that seems to have no end.

Paris and Vincent Landry (Oil and Oil)

Paris was born into one of the most prominent families in Montgomery Valley. She is smart, athletic, and pretty; however, her looks as a child were pale in comparison to her present beauty. She competed in local and state beauty pageants, always winning first or second place, including the title of Miss California and first runner-up to Miss USA. There is a presence that cannot be denied, and every woman of integrity must acknowledge her statuesque beauty. She looks as if her body had been poured into a mold of perfection and skillfully crafted, and she is the epitome of beauty, class, and grace inside and out.

She did not like being an only child, and her dream was to have a large family with three children, two dogs, and maybe a cat, but it was not winning beauty pageants. Her father was a regimented and impersonal military corporal, nineteen years older than his wife, Mary Ellen. She was a quiet, petite, and completely subservient woman who gave birth to Paris at the age of twenty. Paris disliked the way her mother buckled to her father's every command and wished she would stand up and say no, just once. Nevertheless, Paris loved them both.

Paris met Vincent Landry at a "twenty-five hundred dollar per plate" fundraiser held at the Valley Inn Private Yacht Club. She was the guest of the mayor and his wife, Sandy. At these affairs, the mayor always dealt with politics, while women she did not know or like entertained her. On this particular occasion, Sandy invited Paris, who arrived strategically late, wearing a red off-the-shoulder Vera Wang designer dress. Only a blind man could not see her beauty, but he could certainly sense her presence. She literally owned the moment, and he seized the opportunity before anyone else. At this point, his past no longer mattered.

Vincent was a divorcee who was devastated when finding out that his wife had been unfaithful. The divorce procedure was long, bitter, and costly. He developed a strong mistrust of women. He was the father of three children, and one week after the divorce was finalized, he had a vasectomy, vowing never to remarry or bring another child into such a cruel and evil world.

Vincent was eighteen years older than Paris, and their wedding ceremony was one of the most elaborate weddings ever held at the Yacht Club. They were committed to a successful marriage. It was her first, and she promised him she would be the best wife and life partner possible. With Vincent, she had everything she wanted, specifically being treated as his equal.

Vincent understood her desire for children, and Paris married him, respecting his decision not to have more. She was an excellent stepmother despite the closeness of her age to his oldest daughter. Vincent saw the emptiness in her eyes each time the children returned to their mother. On their third anniversary, he had his vasectomy reversed, and they entered a fertility treatment program. After three failed in vitro fertilization attempts, they decided to stop and allow nature to take its course.

Harry and Katrina Maddox (Vinegar and Vinegar)

Harry James Maddox grew up in suburban Chicago, in a typical middle-class family, with two older sisters who adored him and a younger brother who worshipped him. Even as a child, he felt special, perhaps entitled, but by Montgomery Valley standards, he was still vinegar.

He graduated at the top of his high school and college classes and valedictorian of his dental class. He was well known for his painless techniques and was requested more often to perform procedures at the free dental clinic. No one understood how he performed the same procedures under the same professors but always came out smelling like a rose. He was affectionately called Sweet Fang.

Harry met Katrina Witherspoon in high school. She was a sixteen-year-old junior and was the most beautiful girl he had ever seen. It was love at first sight, and he felt it was his destiny to marry her one day. In October of his senior year, they began dating and remained exclusive for the next fifteen months. Going to colleges on different ends of the country put a strain on their relationship, and life became cruel, almost unbearable, when Katrina sent Harry a "Dear John" letter in her freshman year. She explained that they were much too young to have made such a binding commitment and should explore other options. Crushed and heartbroken, he respected her wishes. Five years later, bumping into her at a shopping mall, he was determined he would never let her go. They married three years later and relocated to Montgomery Valley.

Natasha Campbell (Vinegar)

Natasha Campbell was the second oldest of six children born to a single mother on federal assistance and the most sour and bitter portion of the vinegar. Janet, Natasha's mother, gave birth to her at age sixteen. Determined to find a father for her children, she made the same mistake, child after child, possessing the ill-fated talent of selecting the wrong man. Her significant others (or uncles as they were known to Tasha and her siblings) hung around long enough to impregnate Janet, then disappear just before or right after the baby's birth. Tasha's father was the first and set the prototype for Janet's expectations. She watched her mother become more disenchanted and angrier with each man.

By age ten, Tasha was determined her life would be different and she would be the one to break the chain of giving her body to every man promising to love her. She would get an education and use it as her ticket out of this godforsaken ghetto and off welfare. She was called names such as Miss It, Miss Too Good, Miss Goody

Good, Smarty Pants, and with age, Snooty Bitch. They were hurtful, but she developed a resistance to the pain by embracing the thought that the last laugh would be hers. Somehow college would change her direction, and one day they would read about her. That is if they ever learned to read.

Tasha was wise and facing an uphill battle. Her tenacity paid off, graduating at the top of her class and receiving a full academic scholarship to Harvard. After graduation, she was offered an opportunity to attend Yale, but remained at Harvard. Prior to completing her MBA, the top Fortune 500 companies were courting her. She declined offers from some of the most prestigious companies to accept a position with Bethel Industries, LLC, in Montgomery Valley, a young and upcoming company where she planned to become the breakthrough queen.

Linda Marie Black (Rancid Vinegar)

Linda Black, a product of Boston's inner city, grew up in the midst of racism, fighting daily to survive and hoping for respect. She was the vinegar that became rancid during processing and thrown out before bottling. She was the oldest of three girls and wanted desperately to protect her sisters, Gail and Melanie. She realized early that the opposite sex was attracted to her. At five, a boy not much older than she who wanted to get into her panties pulled up to her on his bicycle. He had a butter knife, but she took no chances; it was still a knife. She said no to his advances and began running. It took him a few moments to mount his bike and follow her. She ran as fast as her little legs would take her in the opposite direction of home, not wanting him to know where she lived. She ran toward a barbwire fence, a spot where he could not take his bike and had no choice but to climb it, cutting the back of her calf as she jumped to the other side. With her leg bleeding, she found refuge behind a damp, dingy, and rundown garage for what seemed like hours, breathing quietly so her would-be attacker could not find her. She remained until the darkness surrounded her, and she felt safe enough to run home. She told no one, cleaning and bandaging the wound the best she could.

At seven, Linda asked an adult neighbor to help lift her bike from a storage rack in the narrow dim hallway of their building, something he had done many times. She thanked him, and jokingly he said, "All that work done made me real thirsty. You thirsty?"

She responded, "No, sir, but thank you."

Upping the ante, he offered her a popsicle. A real sucker for a red popsicle on a ninety-degree day enticed her to follow him through the door that opened directly into his musty and cramped kitchen. Taking the popsicle and ripping off the paper, she began licking it. Just as quickly, he pulled her fragile and petite body into his, holding her tightly as he wrapped his thick crusty lips over her nose and mouth. The force of his hard, slimy tongue pushing its way down her throat—coupled with the smell of his foul, sour breath—made her gag. As she struggled to loosen his grip, she dropped the popsicle, hearing it hit the dirty kitchen floor. She was powerless. He heard her whimper, felt her body quiver, and could taste the salt from her tears. This was a turn-on for him. He held her even tighter, and the harder she cried, the more he enjoyed it. Her tiny body began to tremble uncontrollably, which frightened him. She was hyperventilating and unable to breathe. When he let go, she fell to the floor. He thought she was dying. To add insult to injury, he threw a glass of water on her. She lay there, afraid to move, continuing to act as if she was unconscious.

"All right, bitch. Git yo' black ass up and get outa here. If you blabber 'bout what happened in here today, I promise I'll finish da job. I'll cut yo' throat, and you'd wish you'd never heard of me. Now git da hell outa my place, you little punk ass."

Linda crawled out of the filthy apartment, afraid to move too quickly but afraid she was not moving quickly enough. And again, feeling she had no one to turn to, she never told anyone, fearing future retribution. For the next three years, until the day he was found in the alley with his throat cut from ear to ear, she lived in fear.

Linda had not lived a charmed life. By age fourteen, she was built like a twenty-year-old. There were always catcalls from boys in the hood and from older men who should have known better. It bothered her to attract so much attention. She went out of her way to avoid large crowds. Girls talked about her and were jealous of the attention she received. She dressed down to hide her attributes, but baggy clothes were still not enough.

Linda had become a loner. Although she had much to be concerned about, she chose not to allow the climate of the neighborhood to dictate her life. Two weeks after her fifteenth birthday, around dusk and while walking home alone from the theater, she was approached by a group of boys wearing hoods. Terrified, she froze, not knowing what to do. She looked for a way out, a direction in which she could run, but she was surrounded. All she could hear was, "Take it off. Take it off…" As the fear grew inside, she asked, "Take what off?"

"Bitch, don't play us. Take dem damn clothes off foe we rip um off!" shouted one boy.

"What do you want? Who are you? Why are you doing this to me?" she asked crying and screaming.

"Shut up, bitch, foe we have to shut you up. You been hidin' dat pretty ass long enough. We want some, and we gonna get it. Now, bitch, take 'em off foe we cut 'em off."

Crying, Linda begged them to leave her alone. She was at the mercy of the cold streets of Boston. Her screams could not be heard, and if they could, they would probably be ignored. If you wanted to live, you did not interfere. However, she prayed hard for the Lord's intervention and that her prayer would be answered.

"Bitch, I said do you wanna take 'em off or you waitin' on some rough stuff? Hey, guys, this little cookie like 'em rough. Course… if I cut 'em off, I may cut dat pretty little ass and cause some permanent scars. It's up to you."

As the tears flowed, she thought about her choices. Her life was moving in slow motion, but her thoughts were racing at one hundred miles per hour. Surrounded by six thugs, her chance to escape was less than zero. Each was wearing a hood over his face, making it impossible to identify anyone. As long as she did not know who they were, her chances of survival were greater. Rose, an acquaintance, was raped and murdered four months earlier, resisting a rape attempt. It was never established if she died before or after the rape, but according to the beliefs in her neighborhood, a black girl murdered in the ghetto of Boston, case closed. The police considered their hands tied when no one came forward. Linda did not want to die and believed if she cooperated she might live. Slowly she lifted her sweatshirt over her head, exposing the purple T-shirt.

"Shit, come on, come on… Dat's right. We ain't got all damn day or night," the ringleader said laughing.

Linda, shaking, pulled the T-shirt over her head, feeling the cool breeze hit her body. Quickly, she crossed her arms in an attempt to cover her breast and suddenly felt something cold and sharp in the center of her lower back.

"Do you want me to cut dis braw off yo' ass?"

Trying not to touch the sharp object pointed at her back, she reached behind and slowly unhooked her bra. Completely humiliated, she slipped the straps from her shoulders.

As the ringleader continued to close in, she could feel his hot breath on her neck. The smell of the combination of alcohol and cigarettes was disgusting, bringing back the memories of Phil and the day he stuck his tongue down her throat only eight years ago. Then he said, "Now, take dem off. Let's see dat little pussy. Come on, damn it."

Slowly she grabbed the elastic waistband and slipped her pants down.

"Now, da rest of that shit gotta go… now. I ain't telling you no more," he said in a demanding tone.

With tears pouring down her face, she did as demanded. While listening to their comments, she realized they only wanted what they could take. She was their object, and her fear was their ammunition. She turned that fear into anger, and her anger became her retribution. She would play their game. Completely naked, she began to speak with authority. "Okay, here I am. Which of you wants to be first? Who wants this sweet pussy? Or do two of you want to do me at once? Let's get this shit on the road. I'm as ready as you are. Come on… Which one of you boys wants to fuck me first? Which one wants to eat this sweet little pussy? Come on… come on…"

Linda was no longer crying and no longer begging for her life. She was playing the game they used to trap her. "Come on, which one of you has the biggest cock? I want the biggest first, then we'll move on to the little boys. Who's gonna give me what I want... a big, fat, juicy cock? Don't disappoint me, boys. Which one of you can satisfy me? I don't want any of you if all you've got to offer is a Vienna sausage." She kept talking, never stopping. They looked at her as if she was a lunatic.

They were no longer jeering or taunting her. She had become the aggressor, something unexpected. The thrill was gone. Slowly each began to back away. She heard the group's mouthpiece say, "Dis bitch is crazy. Let's git the hell outa here." She kept her eyes focused on them. Although she could not see their faces, she could see the fear in their eyes. She was amazed at what happened. Standing naked and alone and nervous as hell, she quickly located her pants and sweatshirt, slipped them on, and leaving everything else behind, she ran for her life.

Still unable to identify her assailants, she lay in bed, thinking about every ugly and humiliating detail of that night. She harvested the anger and humiliation even in the absence of rape. Fully understanding the culture of the housing project—and that was if you were still alive after such an ordeal and wanted to stay that way—you kept your mouth closed. The only way to win your independence was to get the hell out, and there were only two ways out, either sneak away in the still of the night or be carried away in a wooden coffin. She never told anyone, fearing daily for her safety.

Chapter 1

Dr. Edward Jones retired after forty years of practicing dentistry. His practice was modest but proficient and certainly adequate to maintain a productive lifestyle in the Valley. Locally bred, he was a loyal, loved, respected, and revered community member. He informed his patients of his retirement and that Dr. Harry James Maddox, a bright and competent young man from Chicago, would assume his practice and patients, if they choose to remain.

Dr. Maddox and Katrina were a breath of fresh air, welcomed with open arms and the red carpet rolled out; however, they were still outsiders. He was young and handsome, and she classy and exquisite. He practiced basic dentistry; he was an orthodontist and was well versed in cosmetic dentistry. His touch was gentle, and his bedside manner impeccable. The practice grew from one hundred patients the first year to over three hundred and fifty in less than five years. His patients admiringly called him Dr. Feel Good because he turned the most complicated dental procedure into a pleasant experience, single-handedly taking the pain out of dentistry.

The Maddox family found peace, happiness, and a place they looked forward to calling home for the rest of their lives. Their daughters, Beverly and Angela, were born in Montgomery Valley and by birth were considered Montgomerians, expected to marry and raise their children in the Valley.

Chapter 2

By age seventeen, Linda stopped hiding her attributes. As a senior in high school, she was sent home every other day for inappropriate dress. She no longer walked out of her way to avoid the catcalls but intentionally walked through them and learned to ignore negative comments from petty females. She decided to use what God had given her to get the things she wanted. She was born in the ghetto and would die in the ghetto, but she would be damned if she would spend the years in between existing and not living.

At eighteen, Linda met Horse the summer before her senior year and was immediately attracted to him, not because he was handsome but because of his popularity and the things he could do for her. She knew little about him but felt lucky to be the one. What mattered were the things she loved—gifts, money, and status. He was a high school dropout who hung around the school canvassing for new clients. They were inseparable. As graduation approached, she thought about what she would do next. Secretarial school had been a dream of hers, but it all depended on what Horse wanted.

Horse, whose birth name was Thomas, was a hustler born without a conscience and enjoyed parading Linda around as eye candy. He felt it was his God-given right to have the most beautiful woman in town as a walking billboard for his business. He liked Linda but was not in love and had no interest or intention of being faithful to one woman.

It was obvious how he got his name. They had sex the night they met, and she thought she would die. He satisfied her sexual fantasies, and she loved him in spite of contracting a venereal disease four times. One month before graduation, while making love, Horse said, "Baby, is dis big fat cock juicy enough for you? It sho ain't no Vienna sausage… is it baby?"

Linda's body jerked instinctively, finally realizing why the sound of his voice had been so familiar. It was the alley. She suddenly hated the sight of him. Sick to her stomach, she ran to the bathroom and stood over the commode, dry-heaving. He walked up wrapping his arms around her waist and asked, "You all right, baby?"

"Sure… I'm all right. Just a little queasy," she said.

"Better not be pregnant?"

"No… no, I'm not," she said and thinking to herself, *That son of a bitch. That bastard. How dare he touch me? All this time… how could I have been so stupid and… so blind? How the hell do I get away from this asshole?*

The following day, Horse was waiting for Linda outside of school. "Hey, baby."

"Hey," she responded.

"Is dat all I git?" he asked.

Not having a plan, Linda kissed him passionately, trying not to show indifference. If she wanted to leave, the decision had to be his and not hers. Until the day before, she planned to marry him. She had to maintain her regular routine, knowing he was never going to let her go. He owned her, and she knew it. In one month, she would graduate and had to figure out what to do next. She asked, "Hey, Horse… I'm thinking about going to secretarial school after graduation."

"You crazy bitch? You thinkin' 'bout what? Who da hell been puttin' dem kind of notions in dat head? You gotta be outa yo goddamn mind."

"What's wrong with me going to secretarial school? What am I supposed to do?" she asked.

"You my woman. I take care of you, den you take care of me."

"How do I take care of you?"

"You my woman, ain't you? I do the decidin', and it's when I'm ready."

"What do you mean?" she asked.

Horse became extremely agitated, striking her across the face. She was petrified and frightened. He had never hit her before. She was unsure of what to do, but smart enough not to strike back, knowing she would never win.

"I thought we were going to get married," said Linda.

"I'm not da marryin' kind. You always knowed dat. What's got into you?"

"Nothing. If I don't get a secretarial job, what will I do?"

"You got the tools to make a lot of money for old Horse… a lot of money, baby, just work what father nature done give you. And you don't have to just do men, women like pussy too."

Linda had heard enough. He would never allow her to leave, not without a fight, and she had not figured out what her escape would be.

Linda could hardly wait for the graduation ceremony to end. She did not hear a word of the commencement speech, anticipating what the surprise might be that Horse said he had waiting for her. She wondered if it could be a designer purse, money, a trip, a diamond engagement ring, a designer watch, what? As soon the ceremony ended, she bolted and went directly to see him. When she arrived, she found another woman snuggled close to him. The shock was overwhelming, but her fear prevented her from voicing dissatisfaction. He introduced her to a beautiful woman named Simone, who was her graduation surprise. Simone was going to teach her how to make love to a woman as he watched. Linda became nauseated at the thought but was trapped. She saw the look in his eyes and knew she had no choice if she did not want to be hurt or killed.

Simone began to undress herself while Horse undressed Linda. She stood naked, feeling like a piece of meat, while Simone admired and surveyed the merchandise. Simone kissed her on the neck and stepped back to study her, circling her repeatedly. She moved in again, kissing her on the neck and then moving to her breast. She kissed one and then the other, before gently putting her right breast into her mouth and feeling Linda's body twitch. Linda closed her eyes, and Simone became the teacher. She made love to her much in the same way as any man, only the touch was more tender and sensitive. She knew all the right spots and just how to manipulate them. Linda wanted to pull away, but Horse enjoyed what he saw. She was afraid not to please him and submitted herself completely. She reached an orgasm twice. The first time she was embarrassed, but the second time, she did not care. She screamed out as Simone caressed her body, kissing her tenderly. Horse began to masturbate while watching and soon joined in, going from Linda to Simone and then watching Simone and Linda. The lesson seemed to last for hours, and when it was over, they were exhausted. It was as if Linda was living a nightmare, one from which she could not awake and one from which she would never forgive herself. They fell into a deep sleep.

Sometime between midnight and dawn, Linda disappeared with fifteen hundred and fifty dollars she had stolen from Horse, a thousand dollars she found in Simone's wallet, and anything she could fit into her purse. It was more than enough to get her far away from Boston and just enough for him to want her dead. No one stole from Horse. No one knew where she went, not even her mother, believing no one really cared.

Linda moved to California and enrolled at Montgomery Valley Community College. She found a job as a waitress and was shrewd enough to maximize tips without compromising her newfound principles. The first year she rented a room at the local YWCA in the lower Valley, and the second year she moved into a modest studio apartment. Six weeks before graduation, she was hired as a secretary at Bethel Industries, LLC, and within three years became the executive secretary to Bill Heisman, CEO of Bethel Industries, LLC, earning a salary comparable to a beginning junior executive. She had proven herself to be an invaluable asset.

She was a confident woman, and each movement of her body was deliberate and commanded the attention of every man she met and the respect of every confident woman. The water fountain gossip eluded that she worked her way to the top in a horizontal position. Rumors also surfaced that many deals were finalized with her assistance. Speculation was high as to what many thought, but nothing was ever confirmed. Linda kept her business to herself and was trusted.

Chapter 3

Natasha Campbell, a twenty-three-year-old Harvard MBA graduate, had just become the highest-paid employee for someone of her age, sex, and ethnic background. Her unprecedented arrival was highly anticipated on the management level. She was considered the best, and Bethel Industries felt she was worth the investment.

Daniel met her at the airport, driving her to the prestigious Montgomery Valley Hilton Hotel in downtown Montgomery. Three hours later, she met with a realtor to view homes and condos. At seven that evening, she met Mr. Watson, Bill Heisman's right hand, for dinner. He introduced her to Amanda, his personal assistant. Amanda spent the next three days showing Tasha the city and the best places to shop. Tasha enjoyed the amenities of a chauffeur, taking nothing for granted. Two weeks later, she settled into her condo on the thirty-ninth floor, with a most spectacular and breathtaking view of the city. Bethel expedited the move in process. She was given a company-owned Jaguar without a chauffeur and was excited and ready to kickass.

Chapter 4

Every employee was aware of Natasha's arrival. She had been the topic of every conversation in every venue from the bathroom to the boardroom. Most looked forward to her coming, but there were some who felt she was too highly paid without having paid dues and cared less. Linda was proud of her as a black woman and looked forward to having someone to whom she could relate. Natasha was being groomed to become the first female vice president of the company, which was the deciding factor when accepting Bethel's offer. Upper management embraced her take-charge but sensitive demeanor.

Natasha was escorted through Mr. Heisman's private office for meeting after meeting. She acknowledged Linda with a nod of respect each time she saw her but was not officially introduced until her third day. "Ms. Black, I'd like to introduce you to Ms. Campbell," said Mr. Watson. Natasha was as beautiful as everyone said and a woman Linda wanted to get to know. Her beauty was understated, hidden behind a wall of shyness and a reserved smile. When they shook hands, there was a bond of comfort and mutual respect. Natasha recognized Linda's inner beauty and a level of confidence that she herself had not yet acquired but deeply desired.

Linda and Natasha were the subjects of a betting pool. The naysayers gambled on how long it would take before the "cat fights" erupted. Each was sexy, confident, aggressive, capable, powerful, and smart in her own right. Up until Natasha's arrival, Linda had been the highest-paid black female in the company. Unbeknown to the masses, Linda was not intimidated by Natasha but excited to have the company.

Tasha spent the next two weeks reading and studying company guidelines and policies, rarely taking time for lunch and cramming in as much as possible. She arrived early and stayed late and was like a sponge soaking in everything, rarely seeing anyone, not even her personal secretary.

Chapter 5

Three weeks later, Natasha finally took a break. Her head was hurting, and her eyes were burning. She did not think she could cram anything else in without screaming and needed to stretch her legs. She bumped into Linda in the hall. "Hello," said Tasha.

"Hello, Ms. Campbell, do you remember me? We met in your first week… My name…"

Tasha cut her off saying, "Of course I remember you. And please call me Natasha."

"And I'm Linda. Welcome to Bethel."

"Thank you so much. I'm on my way to a meeting, but I'd like to get together sometime, and perhaps we can have lunch. Why don't you call me and we can set something up?" said Tasha.

"I'll do that," said Linda. She was excited for the opportunity to talk with a strong female whom she did not intimidate. The following week, they scheduled lunch and had an enjoyable time, so much so that they scheduled a second lunch date. Within two months, they were going to the movies and on shopping excursions, and before either realized it, they had become the best of friends.

Natasha had a brilliant mind. She mastered Spanish and French in college and was now enrolled in Japanese and Chinese classes. Her motto is that it is better to be ready and not have to get ready when an opportunity is presented. After one year, she was selected to participate in an eighteen-month program to study the culture of Japan, as well as their business ethics and techniques. While traveling between Japan and California, she became proficient in the language and practically mastered Japan's best business practices.

Being hired by Bethel Industries was considered a privilege. Employees were guaranteed a salary far exceeding the average, respect within the community and excellent credit everywhere; however, Bethel was also known for being an unforgiving taskmaster. Most enjoyed coming to work, but at times, the atmosphere was structured and competitive to the point of destruction.

After returning from Japan, Tasha made a bold recommendation and, with the approval of Mr. Heisman and top management, instituted a rotating four-day workweek for non-management employees and for all, a child-care facility, a mandatory lunch hour, and the provision of an exercise facility with showering capabilities. The facility offered twenty-four-hour access. Two months later, there was a significant improvement in productivity and moral. Absenteeism was almost nonexistent, and employees were happier and more energetic. Tasha scored big, changing the overall culture of Bethel. Those who were once biased regarding her arrival were now her greatest supporters.

Chapter 6

Cheryl was entering her senior year in high school and looking forward to her seventeenth birthday in two months. She was gorgeous, full of life, bright, popular, and a member of the varsity cheerleading team. Being modest, she liked everything about herself, except her teeth. In fact, Cheryl loved herself more that anyone or anything else. Everyone other than she and her parents saw perfection, and being less than perfect was unacceptable by the Davis family standard, and the apple certainly did not fall far from the tree. Her parents must have been born obsessed with the appearance of appearance. At age nine, Cheryl's mother noticed a tiny gap on the upper right side between the eyetooth and the tooth to the left of the eyetooth. Throughout high school, they insisted she get braces to correct this major imperfection, but her fear of dentist was real. In kindergarten, she fell off a swing and was rushed to a dentist. The only thing she remembered was the pain associated with pulling the tooth, and she vowed never to return to a dentist for the rest of her life.

After receiving a pre-acceptance letter from Brown University in Providence, Rhode Island, the decision became easier. She clearly understood life was going to change forever, and nothing less than perfection would do. Cheryl's Aunt Mildred was a patient and fan of Dr. Maddox's painless techniques and recommended him with a guarantee she was sure he would live up to.

Chapter 7

Cheryl's first visit was absolutely pain-free. The fact that he was charming and handsome was an added plus. She started thinking, *If I were older, he'd be my choice.* She saw his wedding band and felt his wife was one lucky lady. Dr. Maddox's staff was accommodating and scheduled Cheryl's appointments around her many activities.

She had her braces for three months when landing the ideal part-time job. Her financially secure parents were against the idea of her working, but she was promised a full-time internship the following summer if she did well. The hours were not flexible and conflicted with her dental schedule. Torn between her smile and her job, she begged for help.

Her parents hoped it would pass since they felt it was more important to land a prominent prospect for a husband than a college degree. A degree for a woman of their status or pedigree is strictly a conversational piece or wall decoration.

On her next visit, straightforward and wasting no time, she said, "Dr. Maddox, I have a problem and don't know what to do."

"Well, little lady, what's your problem?"

"I've just started the best job of my life, and like, you know, I've been accepted at Brown University."

"Congratulations, that's a very prestigious school."

"Thank you... but this job is like great. I really like it and, like, it pays well, but some of my appointments... well, like, conflict with my work schedule... and... I feel like I'm going crazy... trying to fit in school and, like, work and, like, come to the dentist."

"Hold on… you sound like you have the weight of the world on your shoulders. You are much too young to be burdened by the worries of the world."

"I know, but I guess this is what I like… have to look forward to. I guess this is what it means to, like, grow up and become an adult."

"Now, I didn't say you were an adult. You are growing up, but don't rush it, young lady. As it is, life passes much too fast."

"Dr. Maddox, before I started coming to you… I, like, a… hated going to the dentist. Now that my mouth is full of a bunch of metal, I have to like complete this process. My Aunt Mildred was right, you are painless. But, like… how am I going to stay on schedule? Do you have evening hours?" asked Cheryl.

"No, Miss Davis, my wife doesn't allow it," he said laughing.

"You should. There are probably a lot of people who would like to come… if you took appointments in the evening. There are like a lot of working people out there, like me, who cannot take off to come to the dentist."

"Well, I believe they will find the time to do so if they really want to. I really don't think that is something that I have to worry about right now."

"That's true, but like… I want to and can't…" She sounded very much like a wounded child. "This is my first real job, and like… I have the opportunity to make some real money for school. My parents totally refuse to let me work. They are, like, totally old-fashion. Everybody works nowadays. They say it is, like, more important that I study and make good grades and… and, like, I want to go to med school."

"I see. You're quite an ambitious young lady, and I'm sure you're resourceful as well."

"And that's why I'm willing to compromise and negotiate for better hours," she said. "It's different in my day. We women strive for perfection. When my mom was in school, she didn't need an education. She married my dad."

"Don't you think your theory is old-fashioned? Women have been self-sufficient for a very long time. My wife is well educated but decided to stay home and raise our daughters. Now, young lady, my staff is accustomed to the schedule we have in place. They have families too, some with small children, and their schedules are based around our current office hours. They like it. My wife and kids like it."

"Okay, Dr. Maddox, I'll just have to go around with this humongous gap in my teeth for the rest of my life, and, like, when anyone asks who my dentist is, I'll be sure to mention your name," Cheryl said with a smile.

"Hold it, young lady. Sounds like you're trying to blackmail me," he said laughing.

"Is it working?"

"Let me think about it and see what I can do."

The next day, Dr. Maddox surveyed his staff to see who was willing to stay later. The look he received was so chilling he felt bad for asking. After providing sound reasoning, no one was willing to change, and he thanked them. Later that day, Sally volunteered to come in an hour earlier two or three days a week but was not willing to work later than five. He thanked her. During dinner, Harry broached the subject, telling Katrina about his conversation with Cheryl and Sally's willingness to assist. He then asked her opinion.

"Harry, I'm surprised you'd even consider adjusting your hours. You have a booming and successful practice with more than enough patients. If this little girl can't make her appointments, then she should find another dentist," said Katrina.

"Honey, it's not that simple. She came to me because her aunt recommended me. Her aunt is a longtime patient, Mildred Kennedy. This girl and her parents believe she needs braces. They have encouraged her to do this for years, but she refused because of her fear of dentist. She isn't afraid anymore, and more importantly, she isn't afraid of me. None of my patients are, that's why…"

Sarcastically mimicking Harry, Katrina said, "That's why they call me Dr. Feel Good. I know, dear, I've heard the story a million times."

"But… Dad doesn't hurt, Mom… He never hurt me!" shouted Beverly.

"Thanks, baby. Daddy needed that."

"You're welcome, Daddy."

"Honey, I will only go to the office maybe two days a week an hour early, that's not bad. You are rarely up when I leave anyway. Everything I do is for you and the girls. I could have been an ob-gyn and on-call 24/7. Would that have been better?"

"Right! And we probably would have divorced years ago, that much you-know-what is too much of a temptation," said Katrina smiling. "I love you, honey, and I know you'll do what's best."

"Too much information, TMI, Mom and Dad," said an embarrassed Beverly. They all laughed.

Chapter 8

In June Dr. Maddox opened his office at seven on Tuesday and Thursday mornings. Sally adjusted her schedule accordingly. Cheryl was elated and thanked him repeatedly, believing he was more wonderful than imagined. It was a win-win situation for all.

For the first two weeks, things went incredibly well for everyone except Sally. After voicing concern, Dr. Maddox agreed to pay double time for the hours worked and for any additional hours she might work in the future. As a single mother of two, she was grateful for the extra pay, but after three more weeks, the extra money was not worth the hassle. Getting up an hour earlier and getting the children ready for summer camp had proven too much of a challenge. They were often moody, and the change to their biological schedules was disruptive. She allowed them to sleep in an hour later but was using work time to call home to ensure they were up and that they had not fallen back to sleep and remained on schedule. Twice, she called neighbors, pleading with them to take her children to camp after missing the bus. It was difficult. The last straw occurred when she had to leave work to pick them up, take them to camp, and then return. After five weeks, she was desperate to return to her original schedule. No one else was willing to change, much for the same reasons, and he did not think it was fair to insist. Montgomery Valley was a strange and regimented community. He decided to continue the simple process of adjusting Cheryl's braces alone, at least until she left for college in the fall.

Dr. Maddox enjoyed coming in early and did so four days a week. It allowed him time to gather his thoughts and review his schedule, and it eliminated the feeling of being rushed. Three weeks before Cheryl was to leave for Providence, she experienced severe pain in her upper right jaw. She requested the usual seven o'clock time slot, but because nitrous oxide would be required, she was given an eight forty-five appointment. At seven on the morning of her appointment, Dr. Maddox heard the bell ring.

"Miss Davis, why are you here? Your appointment is not until eight forty-five."

"I know, but I thought if I, like, came earlier and you didn't have a patient, you would see me. I really need to, like, be on time for work. We are, like, at the end of completing a special project, and there's a big bonus, and I want… no, like… I deserve my share. This is really important, and like… I could really use the money," she said.

"But I don't have anyone to assist me, and you may not be able to go to work if I have to pull a tooth."

"Yes, I will. Come on, Doc, please, please start on me now. You don't even have another patient… Please. The pain is like killing me."

"Hard heads make for a soft behind, *like*, that's what my father always said," Dr. Maddox said jokingly.

After taking and reviewing her X-rays, he returned. "Your X-rays show that a wire has broken loose on the braces and somehow penetrated your gum. There had to have been some pain prior to today. This is the first time I've seen this happen. There is an infection in the gum. I will remove the braces and take a closer look at the gums and then treat the infection. I will have to numb the gum with injections. However, getting back to the issue at hand, young lady, it is completely against my principle to administer nitrous oxide and do a procedure at the same time."

"You don't know how?" she asked sarcastically.

"Of course I know how, little lady. I just don't like to. My staff has spoiled me," he said.

"Please do it just this once. I promise, I'll be good… and I won't tell a soul. Anyway, I'm already here and, like, a… I'll just have to sit here until my appointment time anyhow."

"I can't do this."

"Dr. Maddox, you are kidding me, aren't you? Like, this tooth is, like, really killing me, and yes, I did feel some pain before this, but like, I've just been too busy," she said.

"And the state Dental Board would take my license if I administered nitrous oxide without parental consent. No matter how grown up you think you are, you are still under the care of your parents, and they still pay the bill."

"Shoot," said Cheryl. "But they know that I'm here."

"Then let's call them," said Dr. Maddox.

"Very well, let's do it," begged Cheryl, and with the verbal consent of her parents, he agreed.

"You drive a hard bargain. Okay. When we finish, I'll write a script for an antibiotic and pain medication. Have it filled immediately. You should probably go home, especially if you decide to take the pain medication. Take a seat in room 4… I'll be right there."

Dr. Maddox changed into his lab coat, laid out the necessary instruments, rechecked the X-rays, and began the procedure. She looked peaceful as he slanted the chair into a comfortable position. Slipping the braces from her teeth, he placed the mask over her nose and turned on the nitrous oxide. She could feel herself becoming relaxed and giddy. As she breathed through her nose, she began to hum softly. Dr. Maddox felt himself becoming aroused while listening to her voice, and it scared the hell out of him. It was totally out of character as he struggled to shake the feeling.

Looking at her reminded him of a young Katrina, and it made him reminisce about the first time they made love and how soft and smooth her body felt against his. He wanted Cheryl right now and was ashamed of his thoughts. She was his patient and a very young one at that. As she continued to relax, she excited him even more. Her breasts were firm and perfect. He fought the desire to raise her top to get a better look. Her skirt fell just above her knees with a surprisingly provocative slit on the right side, especially for a girl of her age. Her legs were slightly parted, but not enough to determine if she were wearing panties. She continued to hum softly, and the sound of her voice intrigued him even more. He was ashamed that a girl only a few years older than his daughter caused his penis to become erect. His thoughts had certainly crossed the line of professionalism.

Harry left the room, thinking only about his family and the great life they have. Katrina was not a prudish lover and was open to everything except anal sex. The one time he mentioned it out of curiosity, she told him she refused to be mounted like a dog and poked in the ass. He respected her decision and never brought the subject up again.

Thirty-five minutes later, the procedure was completed without incident. Cheryl was alert and unaware of his thoughts. She looked at her watch, thanked him, and hurried for the door.

"Don't forget to have the prescription filled before the numbness wears off. We'll put the braces back on after your gum heals."

"Thanks so much for everything, Dr. Maddox. You're my hero," mumbled Cheryl.

When Cheryl closed the door, Harry picked up the phone and called Katrina. "Good morning, sweetheart. Are you out of bed?"

"Not yet. The girls are still sleeping. I just thought I'd lie around a little longer and get some much-needed rest."

"I miss you, and have I told you lately that I love you?"

"Not lately. What's gotten into you?" asked Katrina.

"You're into me. Let's do something special tonight and have a date night. We've not done that in a while. Get someone to stay with the girls, and I'll make reservations," said Harry.

"Okay, sweetheart. But you do realize the girls are old enough to stay by themselves, especially since we are not planning to be out all night? Are we? See you later. Love you."

"Love you too."

Katrina hung up the phone, thanking God for such a loving husband.

Chapter 9

Natasha was at the height of success having done more in two and a half years at Bethel than most do in a lifetime. However, there were two promises she needed to fulfill. The first was to get her unmarried mother, Janet, and her six siblings out of the housing projects. While in Japan, her mother managed to have another child. Natasha felt strange being twenty-five with a one-year-old brother. She told Linda that her first act of kindness was to find a way to tie her mother's legs together, permanently. Janet was forty-one with little to show.

Six months later, she moved her family into the home of their dreams in the suburbs. Tasha agreed to pay the mortgage but required that each adult occupying the home be responsible for paying the taxes and all other bills. It was now time to fulfill her personal dream of getting braces. There had always been one excuse or another to stop her from researching a dentist. She was given the names of three, but only one came with glowing remarks, and that was Dr. Harry James Maddox on Montgomery Boulevard.

Chapter 10

A sharp, intense, and almost paralyzing pain in her left jaw awakened Paris, rendering her sick to the stomach. She looked in the mirror at red swollen gums and knew it was an abscess. It was six thirty, and Dr. Bennett's office would not open until nine. She crawled back in bed and prayed for at least another hour of sleep to block out the pain. Without relief, she was going insane. She called his office.

"Good morning, this is Dr. Bennett's answering service. How may I help you?"

"Yes, this is Paris Landry, and I have an emergency. I have to see the doctor immediately. I believe I have an abscess," said Paris.

"I'm sorry, Mrs. Landry, but the office is closed. You'll have to call back during regular office hours… or I can take a message and have someone call you as soon as they arrive."

"I need to see someone now," she said with a demanding tone.

"I'm sorry, Mrs. Landry. I will call the doctor, and he will return your call. Or you may choose to go to the nearest emergency room."

"Thanks a lot. Please have him call me now. I am in pain!" screamed Paris as she hung up the phone. She called her friend Gloria.

"Hello."

"Hi, Gloria. I know it's early, and I'm sorry to call you at this hour, but I'm desperate. I have an abscess. My tooth is killing me, and I've got to do something *now*! My dentist doesn't open until nine, and I don't think I will last that long. Your dentist, what's his name?" asked Paris.

"It's Dr. Maddox, and he's really very good. His office should be open now or within the next few minutes. It's almost seven, and it's my understanding he sees patients early a couple days a week," said Gloria.

"Do you think he'll see me on such short notice?"

"You can always call and see."

"What's the number?"

"It's 555-354-6664."

"Thanks, I'll try right now! I'll get back with you," said Paris.

Within thirty minutes, Paris was sitting in Dr. Maddox's chair. At eight forty-five, Dr. Bennett returned her call, but she was not available to answer the phone.

Paris was striking even in an old tee and blue jeans. Her dark hair fell to her waist, and she wore it parted, slightly covering her right eye. She was soft-spoken and inwardly shy. Extending her hand, she thanked him for seeing her so quickly. She would have been grateful for a butcher if he could have offered relief. Directing her to the chair in examination room 4, he could not take his eyes off her, noticing her every move.

Harry asked permission to use a small amount of nitrous oxide to relax and decrease her anxiety. Her X-rays confirmed an abscess, and she was given a prescription for antibiotics, one for pain and an appointment for a root canal. Paris was impressed with his demeanor, technique, and bedside manner.

Dr. Maddox scheduled her root canal during normal office hours, but she was adamant about scheduling a seven-o'clock appointment. It was against his better judgment, but not wanting to chance she might not return, he agreed.

Paris arrived at seven sharp just as Dr. Maddox was arriving. He unlocked the door, reached inside, and turned on the lights. He stepped back to allow her to enter. "Good morning," he said. "You practically beat me here."

"Good morning," said Paris.

"How has that tooth treated you?"

"It's been fine. I'm pleased at how quickly the pain stopped. The drugs helped a lot."

"It was penicillin, and the infection caused the pain. You'll be fine as soon as the root canal is done."

"I've never had one. I'm from the old school, just get them filled and keep on pushing."

She entered unbuttoning her sweater and letting it slide from her shoulders. There was a seductive tone about the way she walked and the way the sweater slid down her back, exposing a form-fitting skirt and her beautiful legs. He closed the door, locking it, but Paris did not notice.

"Please, Mrs. Landry, hang up your sweater and take a seat in room 4. I'll be with you in a moment."

Harry pulled off his suit coat, put on a white lab coat, and walked into the room. Her skirt had risen about three inches, and her legs were bare, long, and shapely. She was wearing black high-heeled mules. Her blouse buttoned in the front slightly, revealing her cleavage. He became aroused. It was strange feeling this way. Cheryl and now Paris. He repeated to himself, *Control, practice control.* He washed his hands and, trying not to look, placed the patient bib across her chest. With her assistance, he quickly made the mold for her permanent tooth.

"Now, Mrs. Landry, I'm going to slant the chair so I can take a good look at that tooth."

"Please, Dr. Maddox, call me Paris. I'm not into all the formality. Paris is just fine."

"Okay, Paris… it will be," said Harry. "Open your mouth real wide. Okay, that looks much better. The infection is gone, and we can begin the root canal. Are you ready?"

"I'm as ready as I'll ever be," said Paris.

"I'll give you just a little nitrous oxide, enough to relax you. You should be awake or in a twilight state throughout the procedure, but you won't feel anything, I promise. I'll numb the area around the tooth before giving injections. Are you okay with the nitrous oxide? Otherwise, we can go with injections only."

"I don't want it to hurt, and I hate that drill. Do what you think is best, Doc."

"Just relax, I'll give you just a little," said Harry, placing the mask over her nose. He looked at his watch, and it was almost seven twenty. He waited as she relaxed. The procedure would take at least an hour. After five minutes, he noticed her right shoe had slipped from her foot. He found this incredibly sexy. He was always attracted to women with dainty, attractive, and well-manicured feet. He picked up her shoe, and a sedated Paris smiled from beneath the mask. Lifting her leg, he gently replaced the shoe on her foot and found himself inadvertently stroking her leg as he lowered it. He quickly moved away and retreated into his office. He had the sudden urge to make love to his wife and called home. "Katrina, sweetheart, what's for lunch?"

"What's up, baby? What do you want for lunch?" asked Katrina.

"I want you. I want you served hot and steamy… ripe for the picking. I'll be home at twelve fifteen on the nose. Be ready."

"Harry, what brought all this on?"

"You, baby, I can't help myself. When I think about you, I get turned on. Got to run, got a patient in the chair. See you at twelve fifteen sharp," he said, hanging up and returning to the examination room.

Paris was completely relaxed. He slipped on a pair of latex gloves softly saying, "Turn your head toward me."

Paris turned her body slightly, and the patient bib shifted, falling to one side, once again exposing her cleavage. Harry repositioned it and refocused. The only thoughts running through his mind were related to the root canal.

Harry scheduled her next appointment one month later at the same time. Wondering if he could trust himself and feeling reluctant, his desire to see her overrode his better judgment. He was determined to win her confidence. After reviewing the results of the X-rays with her, he discussed redoing some of her earlier dental work. Secretly, he thought some of Dr. Bennett's techniques were barbaric. At seven fifty-five, he unlocked the door.

Katrina was waiting when Harry got home. They spent the next hour making passionate love, and Katrina was impressed. "Honey, it's been a long time since you've made love to me like this. It took me back about fifteen years," she said.

"Oh, baby… it just goes to show you how much you still turn this old man on and just how much good lovin' I still have in this yardstick."

"Hey, you better get your hot ass and broken ruler back to work. There is a sandwich in the fridge you can eat on the way back."

"Thanks, babe. You always think of everything. I think I'll keep you."

"Hell, you'll have to. No one else wants your old behind, and one that comes with two children and a whole lot of alimony. I'll make sure your handsome little ass will be too broke to leave. Love you!"

Chapter 11

Harry had been looking forward to Paris returning for a month and arrived at the office at six forty-five, fully expecting her to be on time. His plan was to get her treated quickly and out of his office equally as quick. As predicted, she rang the bell at seven sharp, and he unlocked it, letting her in, and immediately locked it behind her. This time she noticed.

"Why did you lock the door?" asked Paris.

"Habit. It's a safety precaution when staff is not present," he said.

"It makes sense, and it's still dark outside."

"And that's another reason. Pull off your coat and have a seat in room 4." She had a butt like Jennifer Lopez, and someone had obviously poured her into her yoga pants. She wore a short knit cropped top exposing her midsection. He was hot and bothered and went into his office to cool down.

After five minutes, he returned and placed the patient bib over her chest and the mask over her nose. "You really don't need the nitrous oxide today. I'm simply removing the temporary and replacing it with the permanent crown. It's not painful."

"I feel fine, Dr. Maddox, but I'm not ready to go cold turkey yet. If you don't mind, just give me enough to relax me. I dislike pain, even the thought of pain. Do we understand one another? Now give me the gas!" said Paris.

"Seriously, Paris, you don't need it," said Harry.

"Just give me a little. Please just a little," she begged as she began to hyperventilate.

"Calm down. Everything will be fine. Just relax."

"I don't know why I'm so afraid," she said.

"Okay, just a little to relax you," he said tilting the chair back as far as it would go. "Okay, Paris, let's take a look. Just relax. It will only take a few minutes to feel the effects."

As he waited, he believed he saw her nipples harden and her legs part slightly beckoning him. He became aroused, and his sexual fantasies raged out of control. He closed his eyes to force back the thoughts running through his head. *I must be going mad. No, I know I am going mad.* It was as if someone or some power was controlling him, and he increased the nitrous oxide, rendering her into a deep state of relaxation. He lifted her top, exposing her bare breast, and was unable to stop.

"Well, what's the verdict, Doc? Is it over?" asked Paris. "I don't remember a thing. That gas really eases the pain."

"Things went well. Let's check your bite. Now bite down and rub your teeth from side to side." The crown was perfect. "Your X-rays revealed decay under two of your older fillings. It may not bother you now, but give it a little time and you'll notice tenderness. I suggest you consider having them capped to avoid losing them completely in the future."

"Boy, I'm not sure I wanted to hear that, but that's why you're the doctor and I'm the patient. When should it be done? How soon," asked Paris?

"There's no rush. After this one is complete, we can talk." Harry hesitated before asking the next question. "How do you feel?"

"I feel great. Why do you ask?"

"I wanted to make sure you had just enough nitrous oxide to relax you but not too much to overdo it."

"Oh, that wasn't too much. It was perfect. I don't remember anything. Let's just do it. I've been with Dr. Bennett all my life, my parents and grandparents as well. He's going to retire soon, and I'll need a dentist," said Paris.

Harry was not sure if he felt guilt or relief. Just as Paris was getting out of the chair, Harry looked down and noticed a wet spot on his slacks and immediately buttoned his jacket to cover it. Unsure if he could get through the day without anyone noticing his buttoned jacket, he decided to go home during lunch to change. However, she planted one sobering thought on his mind. It would only be a matter of time before Dr. Bennett retired, and with luck, Harry could double his patient base.

"Good… I aim to please. I need to see you in about a month."

"Same time?" she asked, cutting him off. "Right?"

"Yes, absolutely," said Harry.

Thirty minutes before lunch, Harry asked Sally to bring him a cup of coffee. When the office was free of patients and the coffee had cooled down significantly, they heard him scream, "Oh shit! I've just spilt coffee all over myself."

That night, his thoughts were all about Paris—her walk, what she wore, and how great her breast felt inside his mouth. When Katrina climbed into their bed, she felt his state of arousal. "Oh my goodness, baby. I just got here. You must be pretty horny tonight?"

"You always turn me on. Just thinking about you arouses me." They made love for over an hour, and every minute, he imagined he was making love to Paris. Even as he drifted off to sleep, he wondered what it would be like to actually make love to her.

Chapter 12

The following month, Harry arrived at six forty-five, convinced that what happened before would never happen again. Paris rang the bell at seven o'clock sharp, and his heart raced out of control, feeling just like a kid on Christmas rushing to open up that first gift. He opened the door and immediately locked it, and this time she did not ask why. "Good morning, Mrs. Landry."

"It's Paris remember?"

"Yes… Paris. Please hang up your coat and take a seat in room 4."

"Yes, sir," she said.

Her skirt stopped just above the knee, and the low-cut scooped-neckline blouse was calling his name. He was becoming aroused. Deciding to take precautions in case he failed to practice control he said, "I'll be with you in one moment." Feeling uncomfortable, he went into his office to rearrange his penis and wadded tissue, stuffing it inconspicuously inside his jockey shorts.

"Thank you for waiting," said Harry.

Harry turned on the nitrous oxide and waited, but overwhelmed by her beauty, he increased the volume. Removing the bib, he lifted her top and covered her right breast with his mouth, suckling it and feeling her nipple harden beneath his tongue. He alternated breast, while stroking her thighs until his body exploded, quivering uncontrollably. The tissue in his shorts was soaked with cum and to prevent soiling his pants, he ran into the bathroom and flushed it down the toilet. Rinsing his face with cold water, he looked in the mirror at a complete stranger. He was determined to control the monster stirring inside, but he remained focused on the temptation of her breast. He repositioned her clothing and turned up the volume on the oxygen.

When Paris spoke, he jumped. Catching himself, he asked, "How do you feel?"

"I feel fine, Doc, just fine. How did it go?"

"I was unable to do anything today. I do apologize, but I was examining your gums and noticed redness around the tooth I planned to work on. I apologize but decided to treat the tooth with a topical. Have you noticed pain?" said Harry.

"Not really. A very small amount, but I thought it was related to the abscess. Then what's next?" asked Paris.

"You still need two additional crowns. After that, I'd like to replace your mercury fillings with porcelain. We have time to get everything done. There is no rush, and remember, perfection is everything in Montgomery Valley."

"As long as it is painless, I couldn't care less," she said.

"I think you'll be happy with the results." Paris was happy, and his job was done with ten minutes to spare.

"When do I return?" asked Paris.

"In about a month. The redness will not be noticeable, but don't worry about it. I have caught and treated it early."

"Okay, thanks so much for everything," she said as Harry walked her to the door, unlocking it.

One month later, Paris returned for her next appointment. Harry felt extremely uncomfortable. She was addictive, and being around her caused him to have an immediate erection. He tried hiding it beneath his coat. He detested Paris for becoming his patient, but a part of him was glad she had. He had violated the Hippocratic oath and his oath of fidelity to his wife and God. He loved dentistry and his family, and he wanted nothing to jeopardize all he had built, so he knew what he had to do. "Mrs. Landry, I believe we have completed our work. It was my pleasure serving you, and I hope you are satisfied with the quality of service provided."

"Remember, Dr. Maddox, it's Paris. I thank you, but I thought you said I needed two more root canals? What happened?"

"Well, eventually they should be done, but it's not necessary right now. Your smile is beautiful as it is."

"Thank you, Dr. Maddox," said a perplexed Paris.

"Thank you, Paris. Call me in the future if you need my services. I know you came to me during an emergency, so I do understand that you will return to Dr. Bennett. He is an excellent dentist, one I highly respect. Have a great day."

"So why am I here today?" asked Paris.

Trying to figure out an intelligent response, he said, "Well, I wanted to check the crown and the redness I saw on the last visit. I also wanted to make sure I had fully addressed your concerns."

"Yes, you did, I guess. Okay… thank you."

"After Dr. Bennett retires, feel free to contact the office, but I don't want to appear unprofessional, as if I'm taking patients from another dentist."

"If that's the way you feel. However, it really is my decision if I want to change dentist or not. Thank you so much," said Paris. She was unable to make sense out of what just happened.

Chapter 13

After more than three years, Natasha finally found time to take care of herself and fulfill her lifelong dream. She made that call. "Hello, my name is Natasha Campbell, and I'd like to make an appointment to see Dr. Maddox."

"Good afternoon, Ms. Campbell. Are you currently a patient of Dr. Maddox?"

"No, I'm not. I was referred by a friend," she said.

"What type of insurance do you have?" asked Maggie.

"John Hancock," she replied.

"Are you the policy holder?"

"Yes."

"And what type of services are you looking to have done?" asked Maggie.

"I want to be fitted for braces," said Tasha.

"Have you worn them previously?" asked Maggie.

"No... but I certainly need them," she said.

Maggie chuckled. "Okay, that's what we do. The first visit will take an hour. Let me see. As a new patient, the wait is about one month. But let me double-check." Perusing through the appointment schedule, she saw a cancellation. "Oh, Ms. Campbell, we've just received a cancellation for next Thursday at one fifteen. Is that good for you?" asked Maggie.

"Oh... that's tough. I'm in the middle of a special project, and I hate to have to take off right now, if I can avoid doing so. Do you have anything later in the day?"

"Let me see. I believe I can move one patient up to that cancelled slot and fit you in at three forty-five? That's the best I can do, and if that works, you need to arrive fifteen minutes early to complete paperwork. We don't normally schedule new patients after three thirty. Let me double-check." Maggie placed Tasha on hold, returning two minutes later. "Yes, thank you for holding. Can you be here by three thirty?" asked Maggie. "I'm afraid that is the very best we can do. Otherwise, his next available appointment is in six weeks."

"No, that's fine. I'll take it. Thank you so much for your help. I really appreciate it. I'll see you at three thirty sharp," said Natasha.

"We will see you then," said Maggie.

"Thank you," said an extremely elated Tasha.

Chapter 14

A determined Paris attempted to schedule an appointment one month later for a root canal. Her seven-o'clock Tuesday-morning slot was taken. Then she requested Thursday morning, and that was filled as well. Rather than return to Dr. Bennett, she conceded, accepting a three-fifteen appointment.

Maggie went into Harry's office to discuss the call. "Dr. Maddox, there was a call from a Paris Landry. She wanted a seven o'clock appointment, but I told her it was already taken."

"I thought she was returning to Dr. Bennett. I took care of her immediate concern. When did you schedule her?" asked Harry.

"We have an opening on next Tuesday at three fifteen. She insisted on an early morning appointment, but I kept telling her they were taken. She acted as if she didn't understand a word of the English language."

"Well, you did the best you could. Thank you, Maggie. And she is intelligent, but loves her early morning appointments, that's all." Harry was disappointed with the three-fifteen time slot and equally frustrated with the thought of her returning. He was ashamed that he was looking forward to seeing another man's wife. His staff had not met her, and he wanted to keep it that way.

Two days later, Harry called Maggie into his office. "Maggie, I have a conflict on Tuesday with Mrs. Landry's and Mr. Thomas's appointments. My doctor is going to a medical conference and has rescheduled my appointment for three. We need to reschedule the two of them." Pausing he asked, "What does my schedule look like for the rest of the week?"

"You're booked solid. I don't know where we could fit them in."

"I hate this, but would you please call Mrs. Landry and ask if she's available for an appointment at five?"

"In the evening? Doc, you are kidding? And what about Mr. Thomas? Do you want him to come in at five in the morning on Monday?" asked Maggie with a tone of sarcasm.

"Yes, in the evening, and regarding Mr. Thomas, he is quick. If you can squeeze him in on Wednesday morning, that would be great," said Harry.

"But, Dr. Maddox, we all leave at five. Don't you need someone to assist you?"

"No, I manage in the morning, and I assure you I'll do just as well in the evening. Thank you for asking. I know I can count on you if needed."

"Sure can," she mumbled under her breath while walking away. "And I sure hope you won't ask," said Maggie.

Maggie called Paris and then returned to report to Harry. "Dr. Maddox, I've called Mrs. Landry, and she's willing to come, but can't get here until five fifteen. Is that okay?"

"Yes, let her know that will be fine." It was perfect. He said to himself, *This is better than expected. They will surely be gone by five.*

"And Mr. Thomas said he can come on Wednesday at eleven forty-five," said Maggie.

"Thank you, Maggie. I knew I could count on you to work it out."

Chapter 15

An elated Tasha arrived precisely at three thirty, and after completing the paperwork, she was taken immediately into examination room 2. Skyla placed the patient bib across her chest, took a full set of X-rays, and developed them before three fifty. At four o'clock, Skyla looked at her watch and knew that if they wanted to leave on time, she would have to keep Dr. Maddox on schedule. Walking into his office, she said, "Dr. Maddox, your four o'clock is ready in two, and it is a new patient."

"Thank you, Skyla. A new patient?" he asked.

"Yes, that's correct," she said quickly turning to leave the room.

"Skyla," he called, raising his voice an octave. "What's his name?"

"Her name is Natasha Campbell. She wants braces. Trust me, by the looks of that mouth, she should have gotten them a long time ago," she said sarcastically in a whisper.

"So she's a dog, uh?" asked Harry.

"Don't ask me, I don't look at women," said Skyla laughing. "No, she is an attractive woman, but by our standards, cha-ching, she is money in the bank! Do your magic, Doc!"

Harry walked into the room and recognized trouble.

"Good afternoon, Mrs. Campbell."

"That's *Ms.* Campbell. Good afternoon."

"What can we do for you today?"

"Put braces on these teeth, please. I've waited my entire life, and my smile has never been my strongest suit. I've developed the art of a very convincing closed-mouth smile. For some reason, my teeth have become more crooked as I've gotten older."

"That's too bad. You are a beautiful young lady, and my job is to help you feel the best you can about yourself. Now, let me see that smile."

His heart melted when she smiled. She was a beautiful, petite, and well-put-together young woman, built like a brick shithouse. Her youth, beauty, and innocence intrigued him. Her gray knit dress had a slit on the right side, and he could see just enough leg to become curious and aroused. Her complexion was a golden bronze, her face smooth and flawless. Her dark-brown hair shimmered with highlights and fell just beneath her shoulders, reminding him of corn silk. He enjoyed running his fingers through Katrina's hair and inadvertently stroked hair from her face. She jumped, and he apologized, explaining it was a natural reaction being in a house full of women. It was becoming difficult to separate reality from fantasy. Her lips were perfect, not too thin nor too thick but just right for kissing, something that never crossed his mind before today.

As her eyes followed him around the room, he became excited. He tried focusing, but it was difficult. The occasional sound of Sklya's voice kept him grounded, and he completed the exam within fifty minutes.

"Well, Miss… Ms. Campbell, we have some work in front of us. All four of your wisdom teeth must be extracted. They are crowding your mouth and over time have caused your front teeth to become more crooked. That is why you've noticed it gradually." Smiling, he said, "Your teeth are strong but you have two small cavities. You will smile with confidence in no time at all, I promise." He thought she was far too beautiful not to have a perfect smile.

"How long will the process take?" asked Tasha.

"It depends on the amount of work required, but you'll wear braces for about two years. It will be worth it in the end."

"Two years!" she screamed.

"It will be over before you know it. There are many types of braces to choose from, not all are metal like the ones you saw growing up. Your lifestyle will not be interrupted. Work with Maggie, and she'll set up a schedule."

"I can't take a lot of time off work. I'm spearheading a new phase of a project that I've managed for almost two years, and I'm dealing with clients in Japan. What are your hours?" asked Natasha.

"I'm impressed. I see patients on Tuesday and Thursday mornings at seven. However, it will require two appointments to remove the wisdom teeth and will take longer than an hour. We must first eliminate the cause, which are the wisdom teeth. Pulling of the wisdom teeth is the most difficult and painful part of the process. We'll work according to your schedule. Once the braces are in place, the adjusting takes less than fifteen or twenty minutes per session."

"Thank you, Dr. Maddox."

As Natasha left, Harry felt a twinge shoot through his body. It served as a reminder that he had already crossed the line. Nothing could or would ever happen with Natasha.

Chapter 16

Just as before, the night prior to Paris's appointment, Harry was thinking about her—what she might wear, what she might smell like, if she would be wearing a bra, a skirt, or those damn tight yoga pants when Katrina climbed into bed. He was in a state of arousal, and she said, "Oh yes, baby, now that's what I'm talking about."

"You know it's all you, baby. Just thinking about you makes me feel like a beast, and I can't control what my big boy does. Now do what you do, baby." They made love, and it was the best it had been in years. Once again, Harry fell asleep with Paris on his mind.

Harry left the office at three for his fictitious appointment and went home to take a brief nap. Unable to sleep, he lay in bed, allowing his imagination to spin out of control. He freshened up and wrote a note for Katrina: "Came home earlier to rest, not feeling well. Better now. Have a late appointment and will see you when I finish. Love you."

As hoped, the staff left prior to his return. He pulled off his suit coat, put on his lab coat, washed his hands, organized the instruments, and waited, but the time seemed to drag. Paris was always punctual, but five fifteen felt like hours away. A few minutes before her arrival, he went to the window, and as predicted, Paris pulled into the parking lot on schedule. He paid close attention to how she exited the car. First, sticking her left leg out, and when turning to the left, her legs slightly parted. It appeared she slowly and methodically brought her right leg out, as if she knew he was watching. Her skirt was well above her knees. All he saw were legs going all the way up to her waist. Her spiked heels must have been five inches. At exactly five fifteen, the doorbell sounded. Trying not to appear anxious, he took his time opening the door. His heart was racing, and saliva was forming in his mouth like a wild animal with rabies. He was ashamed of himself, but proud of the way he orchestrated this appointment.

"Good evening, Paris. I'm so sorry about the inconvenience, and I appreciate you working with me. My doctor has to go out of town and had to change my appointment. He is normally very accommodating, but… I hope I did not cause you a hardship," said Harry.

"No problem, I do understand. I'm sorry I could not get my regular appointment, but it was taken. I really understand," said Paris.

"Well, we will make sure you are able to get the appointment that works for you, morning or evening… you let me know. I am willing to accommodate my patients. Please have a seat in room 4. I'll be with you shortly." Her skirt rose even higher when she sat down. "I'll be right there," he said. Neither of them mentioned the conversation that took place during their last meeting. He placed the patient bib across her chest, washed his hands, and slipped on a pair of latex gloves. With a fully conscious Paris, Harry made the impression.

Before administering nitrous oxide, he excused himself to get tissue to protect his clothing for fear that his naughty penis might seep semen. He returned and laid the chair back, placing the mask over her nose. He felt compelled to increase the volume and watched as she relaxed. He heard her moan, and the sound heightened his arousal. Harry removed the bib, unbuttoned her blouse, and buried his head in her breast, caressing each with his tongue. Her sounds encouraged him, rendering him incapable of stopping. He felt the flesh of her legs, stroking them over and over. She moaned, and he hoped it was out of instinct, but did not care. He pushed her skirt above her waist, slipping off her bikini panties, and then unzipped his pants, dropping them along with his shorts to the floor, revealing his fully erected penis. The wadded tissue also fell. He lightly forced himself inside of her, moving his body up and down, back and forth until he came.

After ejaculating, Harry seemed completely confused about what he should do next. Remembering the tissue, he picked it up, wiped Paris, and then went into his bathroom to clean himself. He wet towels and returned to ensure he had not left telltale signs on her body. Her small frame was easy to maneuver. He slipped on her panties and repositioned her skirt. Her breast continued to call out to him, and he began to kiss and suck them until he felt her nipples harden and an erection reoccur. He maneuvered them passionately, believing her moans were a sign of approval before exploding for a second time. He was completely spent. Trying to refocus, he had to quickly begin the root canal. He wiped up his cum from the floor, rebuttoned her blouse, and placed the patient bib back across her chest. When the first step was almost complete, he administered oxygen to return her to consciousness.

"How do you feel, Paris?" he asked.

"I feel fine. Are you done?"

"With the first step, yes, I am. You did very well today. I hope you did not feel any discomfort."

"I didn't feel any pain. Thanks."

"The procedure went well. Now, don't forget to take the pain medication I gave you the last time, or you may take Tylenol. You will be fine. Remember not to chew on that side, and your permanent will be ready in about a month. If the temporary breaks or comes off, call the office immediately, and we'll get you in right away."

"Can I make the appointment now?"

"Sure you can." He pretended to study the appointment schedule. "My goodness, Paris, it seems like everyone is selecting the early morning appointments. However, it's not my choice, but if you would prefer to schedule another evening appointment, I'd be willing to accommodate you."

"Oh, that would be great. Then one month from today at five o'clock. Is that right?"

"I look forward to it," said Harry. *One month, so close but such a long time from today. Damn*, he thought.

Chapter 17

Tasha was overjoyed when talking with her mother. "Mom, I've finally done it. I'm getting braces."

"I'm proud of you, honey. I know this is something you've wanted for a long time. I wish I could have—"

Natasha interrupted Janet, "Mom, it's okay. You did the best you could with what you had. I appreciate all you've done. You know, Mom, you've always been there and supported me. You encouraged me, even when you may not have thought my dreams were possible. You were not the cliché mom who always told me that I could do and be anything I wanted, even the president of the United States, but you never told me I couldn't."

"Thank you, baby. I'm so proud of you. There were times I thought you would never get out of the damn projects, but you were my strong child, determined. Look at you now. Lord, you're a big-time executive."

"Oh, Mom, I love you," said Tasha.

"You know I love you."

"I've got to go. I'll call you later tonight." As she reflected over her childhood, tears rolled down her cheeks. She tried remembering the faces of her siblings' fathers and wondered what her father looks like. Did she look like him? Or if she bumped into him on the street, would she know him? Would he know her? And what would she do? It was such a bittersweet thought. She never met the father of her one-year-old brother, Jonas. Just like the others, he planted a seed and moved on. Her heart was heavy for the mother she loved so much.

Tasha's appointment was at four o'clock. Extracting wisdom teeth, especially two, is normally a ninety-minute procedure. Natasha arrived ten minutes early and, feeling like a kid in a candy store, waited anxiously in the examination room.

In the outer office, Skyla, Stephanie, and Maggie were exchanging looks, trying to figure out who was going to stay since Dr. Maddox was running behind schedule. As much as it hurt, Skyla walked into his office. "Dr. Maddox, Ms. Campbell, your four-o'clock appointment is in room 2." Hesitantly, she asked, "Do you want me to stay?"

Extremely disappointed by the offer, he said, "That's up to you. It's not necessary, but if you want, I'd appreciate the assistance." He wanted to kick himself in the ass for being so stupid.

"I don't mind staying, but I do need to pick up Bennie by six. I'll have to leave by five thirty, if that's okay," she said.

"I'm running a little behind. It may be close to four forty-five before I actually start. Why... why don't you just go ahead and leave at five? I'd hate for you to have to stop in the middle of the procedure," he said.

"Okay, But I'm willing to give you as much time as I can," said Skyla.

"I appreciate your willingness, but you do have a life outside of this office," he said with a sigh of relief.

At four forty-five, Dr. Maddox walked into examination room 2. "Ms. Campbell, I apologize for running so far behind. There were a couple of emergencies. How have you been?"

"I'm fine, and I understand. I'm pleased to finally begin the process. My mom is pleased as well. She knows this is something I've wanted my entire life, but we could not afford it."

"I remember you saying so on your first visit," said Harry. "I'm sorry it took you so long to schedule an appointment."

Harry checked her chart for all pertinent information, allergies to medication, and previous reactions to nitrous oxide, and he reviewed the X-rays. He felt nervous and unsure of himself being around her. He could hear his staff scurrying around the outer office, preparing to make their mass exit. This bothered him when he began his practice, and now he was glad they did. To slow down the process even more, he asked questions he already knew the answers to. "Now, let me double-check. There were no allergies to medications or problems with anesthesia or nitrous oxide in the past? Is that correct?"

"That's right."

Following additional questions, he said, "I'll give you just enough nitrous oxide to relax you. Some experience a twilight state, and some people remember everything while others remember nothing. Will this be a problem?"

"No problem, sounds fine. I'm one of those who like to be aware of everything, but I guess I need it to get through the procedure without pain. I don't do pain well. I am more comfortable being in control," said Tasha.

Harry was not sure what to think. She is beautiful, but he sensed trouble. He was keenly aware that even she was not conscious of the real scope of her beauty. She was wearing a belted navy-blue sleeveless dress with buttons down the front. Her legs were long and bare. He felt his naughty penis come to life. He noticed the sweet, soft smell of her cologne, and it was perfect, not overbearing. He placed the mask over her nose and watched as the nitrous oxide took effect.

Harry called her name, but she did not respond. He removed the bib, hearing only the soft purr as she breathed. He unbuttoned her dress to discover a front-closure bra. Opening it, he began to gently stroke her breasts, kissing one and then the other. He heard her moan. His penis was now fully erect. He felt her body move and convinced himself she was enjoying it as much as he. It was as if he lost consciousness, control, and track of time and was unable to stop. He suckled her entire left breast in his mouth, toying with it, working his way to the nipple, repeating this pattern over and over, alternating from breast to breast as she moaned to his rhythm. The more she moaned, the more excited he became until he exploded. He was worn out and had not penetrated her. He had never seen a more perfect set of breast. When reality set in, he promised himself he would get it together because he had too much to lose.

Harry wet a towel and gently wiped the saliva from her chest, refastened her bra, and buttoned her dress. After making sure everything was back to its original state, he removed the upper and lower wisdom teeth on the left side. It was a textbook extraction. Thirty minutes later, the procedure was complete.

"Ms. Campbell, how do you feel?"

"A little numb and puffy, but I'm all right. No pain yet," said Tasha.

"It took about thirty minutes longer than expected. The root of the tooth was crooked and caused a bit of a problem, but I got it. I had to increase the nitrous oxide to dig deeper into the gum. I did not want you to awaken during the process, it would have been far too painful. Is everything okay?"

"Perfect."

"In about a month, your gums will be healed, and then we'll tackle the other side. Follow these instructions for proper care. If you experience a problem, call the office immediately. Otherwise, call Maggie to schedule your next appointment. Let her know what time works for you." He looked forward to seeing her again.

Unexpected and to Tasha's disappointment, her presence was requested back in Japan. It was a golden opportunity to be able to complete the launch of the program she began initially, and there was no one more qualified to do so. She understood the nature of her job, and to become the first female vice president, she had to do what had to be done even if it included putting her braces on hold for just a little longer.

Chapter 18

Paris felt extremely comfortable with Dr. Maddox, considering him not only her dentist but also a friend and surrogate psychiatrist. She confided in him her desire for children and that she and Vincent could not have them, her relationship to Vincent's children, and the emptiness felt after each visit. She felt no need to share Vincent's story. Harry assumed Paris was infertile, feeling she would have been an excellent and caring mother. Each time she visited, his task became easier. There was no longer a feeling of fear or guilt, only power and entitlement. Her inability to conceive was an added benefit.

Over the next four months, Harry found every possible reason to fix or repair something in her mouth. In search of the perfect smile, she had given him free will over her mouth and unknowingly free will over her body. He performed two crowns and replaced every mercury fillings with porcelain. He cleaned her teeth twice and performed unnecessary whitening treatments.

Paris arrived earlier than usual for her next appointment. She was overjoyed and beaming and could hardly wait to give Dr. Maddox the great news. Enthusiastically and bubbling with excitement, she blurted out, "Dr. Maddox, I'm six weeks pregnant."

Shocked, surprised, and almost dropping to the floor, he forced a smile, saying, "Congratulations! I'm so happy for you."

"Thank you. I only wished Vincent was as happy as I am. We've being trying to have a baby for years. He had his vasectomy reversed on our third anniversary, and all we seem to have had was bad luck. There have been three unsuccessful in vitro fertilization attempts. I can't believe I'm finally pregnant. I'm excited, and he should be also. We've been through so much. The doctor always said if we would just relax and stop trying it might happen. I'm so happy it finally did. I just want him to be as happy as I am." She wanted to share Vincent's story with Harry in the beginning but felt embarrassed for their inadequacies, and it really wasn't something you share with just anyone.

"And you should be… both of you."

"And that's what I thought, but since the reversal, his doctors convinced him that his sperm count was too low. I'm sorry, I know you don't want to hear all of this."

No, I don't, he said to himself as fear ran through his body. *I have been so stupid assuming that just because he already has children that she was the one who was infertile. Could I be the father? Impossible! You stupid son of a bitch!* "But it's important. I can't give you the nitrous oxide to relax you while you're pregnant."

"But I can't go through the treatments without it. I'll go crazy. I can't do it. I just can't do it."

"We can suspend the treatments until after the baby is born. We're almost to the point of completion. Now is the perfect time to stop. We can just wait. The problem teeth are out of the way. It can wait."

"Does that mean you won't do anything today?"

"No, I can't. I have two healthy and beautiful daughters, and don't want to chance harming your baby. As much as I hate to stop the progress we've made, I feel it's best. Just call after the baby is born." Begrudgingly and again he said, "Congratulations and good luck."

"Thank you, Dr. Maddox. You know I need the gas." She smiled and waved good-bye, heading for her Jaguar.

He watched closely as she left. He always looked forward to seeing her and was disappointed by the news despite her jubilation. However, he was scared shitless. He just wanted the pregnancy to be over and prayed he was not the father. If so, he would be a dead man in seven and one-half months. Then he dismissed the thought.

When Paris initially told Vincent about the pregnancy, they argued, something they rarely did. He was convinced he could not be the father, and Paris was positive he was. She loved him at first sight, and that love was unconditional. She had been faithful since the day they met and swore to Sandy that she would spend the rest of her life with him, loving him more than she loved herself.

Since the announcement, Vincent had his sperm count tested several times. The type of test needed to confirm conclusively that he was or was not the father could not be done without the consent of Paris. Dr. James explained that medical science is a science, and anything is possible, and unless he had reason to believe Paris had been unfaithful, then he was the father. He loved and trusted her, and she had never done anything to make him believe otherwise, so he put his fears to rest and dismissed all thoughts of having the baby tested. Paris was not the wife who cheated, and he could not make her pay for Carla's indiscretions.

Finally, he embraced the idea of becoming a father again and prepared for their bundle of joy by surprising her with a trip to their favorite place, Paris, France, and the place where they honeymooned. It was where her parents met, married, and conceived her. At birth, there was no greater honor for them than to name their daughter Paris. Vincent could not have selected a more perfect or romantic place. They fell deeper in love and could not wait to welcome their child into the world. While walking down the Champs-Élysées, they tossed around baby names. If it was a girl, Vincent wanted to call her Parisian. Paris laughed at the thought. If it were a boy, they would name him Jacques. Their lives could not be more perfect.

Chapter 19

Natasha was excited to resume the process of getting her braces and called Dr. Maddox's office three weeks before returning from Japan to schedule an appointment. When Harry heard she was returning, he could not erase her image from his mind. Paris was his catalyst for change; however, his attraction to Natasha was terrifying.

Natasha returned to a demanding and out-of-her-control schedule, and once again, her job was given priority. *Damn it,* she thought. It had been eight months, and she was ready for braces. Realizing early the morning of her appointment that there was a problem and not wanting to delay the process further, she called to explain the situation and ask for a later time. Maggie confirmed she could come later. As a safety net, Harry prayed she would arrive while his staff was still present.

Among the staff, there was the typical conversation as to who might remain late, however confident that if they offered he would dismiss them. He confirmed what they already knew.

Natasha arrived at four forty-five, very apologetic. She was quickly prepped and placed in examination room 2. At five o'clock sharp, his staff said good night and closed the door behind them. Harry took a few moments to ensure the door was locked.

"Good to see you again, Ms. Campbell. How are you?"

"Fine, Dr. Maddox," she said.

"How was your trip to Japan? I understand you speak Japanese fluently, is that right?"

"Kyo wa genkideus ka?" said Natasha.

He had no idea what she said, but it certainly sounded sexy. "I am well, thank you," he replied.

"Oh! I thought you did not speak Japanese?" said Natasha.

Harry let out a loud burst of laughter and with amazement said, "I don't, I guess I just lucked up on that one. How are your gums?" he asked, and before she could answer, out of nervousness, he continued, "I'm sure they have healed sufficiently and we can start improving that smile. Now, let me see. Smile." He felt totally stupid asking such an asinine question.

"Yes, it's only been eight and one-half months. I am perfectly healed."

"Did you have problems with swelling, soreness, medication, or anything?" asked Harry.

"None at all. Things went very well. And I have no plans of leaving town before getting my braces," said Natasha.

Harry continued to stare in the direction of the door as if he was expecting someone.

"Let's take a look. Yes, yes, yes, your gums look great. Now we can take care of the other side. Just to warn you up front, since we had problems with the left side, there is a possibility we could run into the same problem on the right side. If so, it will probably take the full ninety minutes to complete the procedure, and I may have to increase the level of nitrous oxide."

"That's okay. I've waited this long, ninety minutes is nothing. I want to get this over," said an exhausted Tasha.

"Now just relax, this won't take long."

Harry watched as the nitrous oxide took its effect, feeling much like a shark smelling blood in water waiting to strike. He watched her body relax, and as his penis became erect, he increased the flow. After five minutes, he called out to her, and she did not respond. He removed the protective bib, calling out once again. He felt excruciating pain in his crotch. He unbuttoned her blouse and unsnapped her front-closure bra. He kissed her breast, first one, and then the other, and began to suck them, gently, then harder, until he heard her moan. He called her name and still no response. He continued to manipulate them with his tongue, softly, then harder, softly and then harder, until he felt her nipples harden. Her breasts were soft and smooth, and her moans intensified the fire already burning within his body. He could no longer stand the pain of suspense and raised her dress, removing her panties. He removed her shoes, revealing perfectly manicured feet, and proceeded to kiss them, not stopping until he had sucked each toe.

Uncontrollably and without caution, he began kissing her sweet spot. She possessed an innocence and purity he could smell and taste. The moaning drove him crazy, escalating his desire to take her. He undressed himself from the waist down and, with a full erection, stood in front of her, no longer possessing the ability to reason between right and wrong. As the room spun out of control, he switched between sucking her breast and tasting her while his body shivered until his penis pulsated to the point of unbearable pain. Although very close to reaching an orgasm, he wanted the feeling to last. He mounted her using his body to spread her legs apart. He was careful not to thrust the total weight of his body on top of her, fearful of causing bruises. He felt how tight she was and gently inserted his penis into her a little at a time, pulling out and pushing in, repeating the process until his penis could go no further. Her cavity was tight and warm, and he felt as if it was pulsating. He continued raising and lowering his body, up and down, back and forth, up and down, until exploding. He let out a loud sound of relief capable of being heard from the street. Spent, he fought for the strength to get up. He had experienced the most powerful orgasm of his life. The condom caught his cum.

Harry went into the bathroom for towels and returned to wipe Natasha clean when noticing blood. *Oh shit,* he thought to himself, *what the hell have I done?* With his heart pounding out of control, he used wet towel after towel until there was no longer any trace of blood on her body or the chair. Scared shitless and feeling grateful, guilty, and scared, he redressed her and kissed her breast one last time before fastening her bra, buttoning her dress, and replacing the bib across her chest. Natasha had already received nitrous oxide for fifty minutes, but he needed a few more. Concerned about the possibility of making a mistake, Harry hurriedly removed the wisdom teeth on the right side. He was grateful for another textbook extraction, and ninety minutes later, Tasha was coming around.

"How are you?" he asked.

"I'm fine. I had so many crazy dreams, one right after another."

Harry, petrified of what she might say, would not ask for an explanation. He said, "Just as suspected, we experienced the same problem on this side. However, we were on schedule, but I had hoped to finish a little earlier."

Natasha looked at her watch. "Is it okay to have nitrous oxide for that long?" she asked.

"You didn't have that much, I kept it light. It just affects some people differently. You were trying to talk during the procedure, and I had to tell you several times not to talk and just let me do my job."

"My lips feel like they are so big. Am I swollen?"

"It's not as bad as it feels. I suggest you apply ice immediately to prevent swelling. Do you still have pain medication left from before? They are still good. If not, I can write another script. And remember to follow the directions provided."

"No, I have enough. Thanks. When should I come back for the braces?" she asked.

"Oh, maybe a month or sooner. Your gums need to heal. You will have to let me know how you feel and when you feel ready."

"I'm ready now. Okay, I'll call for the next appointment."

"I look forward to hearing from you," he said. "Don't forget to use ice, and if you have a problem, call my emergency number."

As she left, he felt many emotions—fear, anxiety, nervousness, and as if he was losing his best friend. He could not put his finger on it, but she caused him an unusual level of concern.

Later that night, Tasha felt a level of discomfort never felt before.

Chapter 20

Natasha lay in bed with the most sickening feeling in her gut, sensing something was wrong. The next morning, she woke up with an unexplainable soreness in her upper thighs and, being a virgin, was not sure why. She spotted traces of blood in her panties and played it off as residue from her last period. She immediately suspected Dr. Maddox had done something to her. She checked her panties for a discharge and performed the smell test, but nothing seemed unusual. She could not accuse him of something she was not sure happened. However, when under the nitrous oxide, she dreamt she was having sex and now wondered if it was more than a dream. Her suspicions led her to confide in Linda.

Linda had been a victim many times but felt a woman as pure and kind as Tasha did not deserve to be victimized. "Tasha, you're my girl, and we have to find out if he put his nasty filthy hands on you. Girl, hell no! I'll check him out. I'll make an appointment. I can smell a son of a bitch a hundred feet away."

"No, don't do that. I don't want you to put yourself in a position to be molested or, in this case, possibly raped," said Tasha.

"I can handle myself, and I can certainly handle any man. Remember, I told you I dated a man named Horse, who was the meanest and nastiest son of a bitch God ever put on this earth. Trust me I can handle some wimpy dentist," said Linda.

"Be careful, this man is probably a pro."

"I will, girlfriend, and I've got your back… that you can take to the bank," said Linda.

Chapter 21

Tasha and Linda spent the next two weeks devising a plan. However, Natasha made an appointment to see Dr. Williams, her obstetrician gynecologist, while Linda scheduled an appointment with Dr. Maddox. His first available appointment was in three weeks. Tasha repeatedly instructed her not to allow him to give her gas, and Linda assured her she would be careful, knowing if she were to get to the truth she would have to allow him to administer nitrous oxide.

Linda arrived early to complete the new patient information forms. Maggie noticed her slinky, catlike, smooth, and deliberate moves. It was obvious Linda was well aware of her assets and knew how to use them. Maggie said, "Whoa, girls, get a look at this hot number. Look at the way she's dressed. What or who is she after?"

"Hey, ladies, aren't we being judgmental? She's probably a very nice woman. Don't be jealous because girlfriend does look good. Don't be a hater," Stephanie laughed.

"Shoot, I used to be a hot little number myself... back in the day," said Maggie.

"How long ago was that?" asked Skyla.

"Shut up, girl. I did have my day," she said. "It does take me way back."

"Yeah, the operative words are *had* and *way back*," said Stephanie. "Maybe we'd better look out for Doc's wife. This woman may be looking for a wealthy man."

"With looks like that, she probably has several and a sugar daddy to boot," said Maggie.

"Hey, you're right, but at any rate, Doc's heart may not be able to take it," Skyla chimed in.

"Doc is a professional and a big boy. He sees beautiful women every day and all day long. After all, he's got three of the hottest divas in Montgomery Valley working right here under his nose, and if anyone was going to turn his head, we would have," said Maggie. They all laughed as Skyla exaggerated her walk to the door to call Linda into room 4.

"Doc, your four o'clock is in room 4. And, Doc, you'd better brace yourself for this one. She's a sassy hot number. Her name is Ms. Black, Linda Black, just like the black widow spider," said Skyla in a voice common to a spooky movie.

Harry's mind went wild imagining how she actually looked. He almost broke his neck trying to sneak a peek without being noticed. Quickly finishing Mr. Scott and walking into the room, he almost blurted out loud, "Holy shit!" Linda was more than expected. Extending his hand and trying not to drool, he said, "Good afternoon, Ms. Black. I'm Dr. Maddox. What can I do for you today?" She was the sexiest woman he had ever seen, and every part of her said, "Take me." Her outfit was a billboard for sex, and it took all of his power to practice self-control.

Linda lost her breath when Harry walked in. Tasha failed to mention how good-looking, charming, and seductive he was. His presence made her feel giddy like a schoolgirl. In a seductive tone, she said, "I haven't been to a dentist in a long time, and I know I need some dental work. I'm sure there's plenty going on in this mouth."

"Is there a particular area causing you a problem? Any pain?"

"No, Dr. Maddox. I have some sensitivity to hot and cold."

"Well, it's my pleasure to meet you. I'm here to make sure all of your dental needs are met. Let's take a look. Open wide." Inwardly he was saying, *I wish it were her legs I was talking about.* "Skyla will take X-rays, and I will return after reviewing them to let you know what I find." Normally all X-rays are taken before he enters a patient's room, but curiosity caused him to jump the gun.

Feeling an erection emerging, Harry readjusted his briefs and buttoned his lab coat. Closing his eyes, he mentally reviewed the black sweater with the low-scooped neck revealing her ample bosom. She was a breast man's dream. He thought Natasha was built, but this woman made her look like a schoolgirl approaching puberty. Her skirt was four inches above the knee, and when she sat down, it rose another three. Her legs were perfect, smooth and well sculptured. They looked as if she had been a premiere ballet dancer. She wore a pair of black ankle-strapped stilettos with a peep-toe. She was a professional in every sense of the word. He had sized her up, knowing she had been around the block more than once. She was well aware of what she had and knew exactly how to use it. Her entire persona spelled trouble, and he knew it, but he had come to love the challenge of being challenged.

After reviewing the X-rays, a hot and bothered Harry returned within twenty minutes. He noticed Linda's eyes following his every move, and that was a huge turn-on. "Ms. Black, I see we have work to do. There are a few areas that need attention. You have six small cavities. You need two root canals, and you are due to have your teeth cleaned. Have you felt any pain in your lower molar?"

"No, I knew there was a problem, especially with sensitivity, so I thought I'd better check it out."

"Who referred you?" he asked.

"I found you on the Internet," she lied.

"Well, young lady, I can certainly help."

"Eventually, I'd love to replace your silver fillings with porcelain, giving you a more natural smile. I'm not saying that your smile isn't already beautiful… I want your smile to match your beauty. We can start immediately. I hope I did not offend you."

"Not at all, Doc. What if I decide to wait?"

His heart deflated, as if someone stuck a spear through it. "The call is yours. I'm at your disposal, and if you decide you want my services, just let me know. You don't want to wait too long. The teeth requiring root canals will eventually become inflamed and cause a significant amount of pain and eventually infection. You don't want to chance losing the teeth. I don't see any evidence of gum disease, but I recommend you use toothpaste for sensitive teeth."

"Just kidding, Dr. Maddox," she said in a somewhat seductive voice.

He could tell she was a natural flirt, and that also turned him on. *Remain professional, remain professional* were the words scrolling in his head.

"What do we do first?" Linda asked.

"The first thing is to clean your teeth and then schedule a series of appointments. Maggie can help you with that. Skyla will clean your teeth, and I'll see you back soon."

"Fine, I'll do that. Looking forward to perfecting my smile."

"Perfect smiles are what we are known for."

"How painful is this process going to be?" asked Linda.

"Cleaning of the teeth... not painful at all. When we began the fillings, root canals, and anything else, there will be pain, but we have something to take care of that."

"Such as?" asked Linda.

"Nitrous oxide. It's just a little gas to relax you," he said.

"Oh, I've had that before when I was a teen. It knocked me out, right out. It doesn't take much for me."

"Would you rather not have it?" he asked.

"No, I want it. I just don't need that much," she responded.

"We'll determine that when we get started. Now, let's get your teeth cleaned and get you scheduled for follow-up appointments. Is that okay?" Harry asked.

"That's just fine," said Linda.

"Ms. Black, before leaving, please be sure to see Maggie."

"Thank you, Dr. Maddox. I'll do that."

Harry could not wait to see her again. She was in and out before his staff made their mass exit. Somehow he would figure it out. He managed before and would do it again.

Chapter 22

Linda called Tasha's cell and left a message after leaving Dr. Maddox's office. "The wheel is in motion. Have a second appointment in two weeks. Will keep you posted. His ass will be toast soon. Girl, you did not tell me that man was so fine! Talk to you later tonight, and love you."

Natasha returned the call after leaving work. "Girl, what happened?"

"You did not tell me the man was so fine," said Linda.

"Shut up, girlfriend. Let's not get it twisted. He is good-looking, but he could be a good-looking low-down dirty son of a bitch. My goal is to expose his ass as a rapist. What did he do? Did he try to give you the gas?"

"No. Do you remember telling me not to let him give me the gas? They cleaned my teeth, and they needed it. I have set up a series of appointments. However, there is nothing later than four. She told the front desk that I work days and do not have a lot of flexibility and requested an evening appointment. The watchdog gave me a four-o'clock appointment, but I know how to handle that. I'll just call and let them know there is an emergency and I'll be a few minutes late. I can always get stuck in this California traffic. Girl, let Linda work it out. I got this, baby girl."

"Are you sure he did not try anything?"

"No, I said I only had my teeth cleaned, and he did not do that. There was an office full of people."

"Okay, do not, I repeat, do not let him give you gas," said Tasha.

"Do I look stupid? I heard you. I need two root canals, and I don't believe I'm strong enough to endure that without the gas. I told him I don't require a lot. That way, he'll give me a light dose, and if… if he tries anything, we'll have him on the spot. I can record the appointment, and he'll never know. I've got your back. Trust me, this is in the bag, and it's a done deal. Leave it to the pro. Remember, I was raised by the streets."

"Okay, girlfriend," said Tasha. "I'll let you handle it. I go back next week for my braces. What should I do? And you can't use a recording in court if the other party did not give consent."

"Just go back. Let me handle this. How many times do I have to say it? Just don't let him give you the gas." Both of them laughed as they said the statement simultaneously. "The plan is in motion. He asked who referred me, and I told him I found him on the Internet. I don't want him to know we are friends or that we work at the same place."

"Good, that's best," said Tasha.

Two months passed before Tasha returned to his office. Harry was happy to see her because her absence made him nervous. He interpreted her return as a sign she remembered nothing. She was stunning, but distant. Feeling a bit safe but afraid to say too much, he allowed her to control the flow of the conversation.

Harry had practically lost interest in Katrina sexually. The girls were at the age where she was playing chauffeur, taking them to dance lessons, soccer practice, gymnastics, Jack and Jill, everywhere, anywhere, always tired and never available. He missed their intimacy, the conversations while making love, but he had become a different person, one who loved being in total control in a submissive situation, doing what he wanted, how he wanted, and reaching higher sexual plateaus than ever.

Chapter 23

At three forty-five Linda called Dr. Maddox's office to explain that she was stuck in traffic but assured Maggie she should arrive within fifteen minutes. Ten minutes later she called again saying traffic was being detoured and she should arrive by four thirty. Maggie, a bit disturbed, suggested she reschedule. Linda, knowing she had already won the war with Harry, refused to lose the battle with Maggie and asked if the doctor could make an exception. After five minutes of back-and-forth conversation, Maggie placed her on hold. "Dr. Maddox, the floozy is on hold. She is stuck in traffic and will be late. I tried to reschedule, but she is determined to come today and wants to know if you could possibly make an exception, as if none of us has a life outside of this office, including you," said Maggie.

"It's okay, Maggie. I appreciate what you do, but we are in the customer service business and should not mind accommodating patients. Who is the floozy, and what time was her appointment?" asked Harry. "Remember, it takes all kinds of customers to keep this office in business and pay your salary, including floozies." He knew exactly whom Maggie was referring to and was cheering on the side of traffic.

"Four o'clock, and it's Ms. Black. I told her she needed to be on time for her appointment."

"Don't worry. I don't have plans for tonight. If it becomes a problem for her to get here, she should be scheduled for one of my early morning appointments." *Yes, God works in mysterious ways. This is better than planned*, he said to himself.

"Sorry to keep you on hold, Ms. Black. The doctor said he can accommodate you. Just come in as soon possible," said Maggie.

"I will. And thank you for all of your kindness!" said Linda sarcastically. She hung up and called Tasha, saying, "Today is the day. I am stuck in traffic and have to take a detour. He is willing to accommodate me, said the watchdog. When I finish eating and brushing my teeth, I should get there by four fifty. I'll call you later this evening."

"Sounds good. Love you, girlfriend, and thanks for doing this. Watch out for the gas," said Tasha.

"I will... I will! Let me handle this. Remember, guys like this raised me. Later." Linda hung up the phone, double-checked her attire, made sure her makeup was perfect, and walked out the door.

Chapter 24

Perfectly orchestrated Linda arrived exactly at four fifty as the staff put away equipment. Skyla quickly ushered Linda into examination room 2 and placed the patient bib across her chest. Linda thought, *Damn, she just covered up my best asset.* Skyla also noticed her exposed breasts, but at least felt her skirt was not as short or as form-fitting as before, a bit more modest.

"Doc, the Black Widow Spider is in examination room 2. She has been prepped. I am leaving shortly. Stephanie had to leave at four, she had an appointment," said Skyla.

"What about Maggie?" asked Harry.

"I'm not sure if she's staying," she said.

"Thanks, I'll be in shortly, and her name is Ms. Black. She is a patient, and that patient helps to pay your salary as well as Maggie's," he responded.

Harry could feel the rush of adrenaline, and his penis began to pulsate just remembering her first visit. *Calm down, boy*, he kept repeating to himself.

"You're right. Good night, Doc," said Skyla.

"Good night, Doc," said Maggie.

"Good night, ladies," said Harry. "And good ridings," he said, mumbling under his breath.

Relieved, he listened to hear the door close. He walked into the outer office, double-checking and securing the dead bolt lock. He looked down to ensure his erection was hidden beneath his lab coat before walking into the room.

"Good evening, Ms. Black."

"Good evening, Dr. Maddox, and I'm so sorry for being late. There was an accident on the freeway, and the traffic came to a complete stop."

Interrupted by Harry, he said, "Maggie told me the story. No problem. I'm glad I could accommodate you." He was tired of wasting time. "Are you ready to take care of the first crown?"

"Yes," she said.

"We will make the mold of the tooth first, and then I'll give you nitrous oxide to relax you. That way, I can use the drill, and you will not experience as much discomfort, but I do remember you don't require a great deal. Is that right?"

"That's right."

"Okay, I never give large doses anyway. Just lie back and relax. Let the doctor do the rest."

Hearing his voice made Linda want to cream in her panties, especially when he said, "Let the doctor do the rest." *What is it he does?* Then she said, "Now remember, I only need a little. The last time I had this, it took over thirty minutes for me to come around."

"I remember. Just sit still and give the nitrous oxide time to work." He watched her relax, wondering how each woman he was attracted to was more alluring than the one before. This one had a dark and seductive mystique about her that screamed his name. He unbuckled and unzipped his pants to relieve the pressure building from within. "Linda, Linda." No response. Having given her much less than normal, he nudged her arm repeatedly while calling her name. He then removed the bib, exposing her ample and velvet-like bosom. Tenderly he manipulated them with his tongue, feeling her nipples harden. He caressed her breast, one in each hand, kissing and sucking, alternating from one to the other. Linda began to moan, moving slightly. He heeded to caution calling her name but continued to pleasure himself. The pain in his crotch was so unbearable he placed his head between her breasts to allow the pain to subside. After catching his breath, he called out again, and she responded only with soft moans. She had awakened every burning desire within him.

"Linda... Linda." He continued to manipulate her breast until he felt her nipples harden once again. She moaned as if she welcomed his advances. He dropped his pants to the floor and removed his briefs. He raised her dress and removed her thong. When kissing her bare sweet spot, it seemed as if she reacted. He thrust his tongue inside of her, feeling her warmth and tasting the sweetness. He mounted the chair, placing one knee on each side of her body while anticipating entrance before remembering he did not have a condom. His penis was hard, burning and begging for entrance. Instead, he sandwiched it between her breasts, moving his body back and forth until he exploded without warning. Exhausted, he quickly caught himself to prevent the weight of his body from coming down on her. With cum spewed over her chest, he looked for a towel, but there was not one. "Linda... Linda." Not knowing what to do next, he began licking her throat, breast, and cleavage, and the more he did, the more she moaned, encouraging him even more. He did not stop until every trace of cum was gone. Having experienced his highest sexual experience and just like an uncontrolled animal with a pulsating penis, he began to suck and fondle her breast again. Finally, looking at his watch, he panicked because ninety minutes had already passed.

Harry splashed cold water on his face, brushed his teeth, and wet towels with warm water and soap. Returning to the exam room, he dressed and proceeded to wipe Linda until he was certain nothing was left to cause suspicion. She moaned with each swipe, further intensifying his desire. Too much time had passed, so he increased the oxygen flow to bring her to consciousness.

"Ms. Black, I don't know how to say this, but I was unable to start the process. I am so sorry to put you through this. You were right, the nitrous oxide does have a powerful effect on you. As I begin the procedure, I realized the drill was broken and the staff had locked up the other drills. I called Skyla and left a message. By the time she called back, it was too late to start. I decided to allow you to sleep off the gas, rather than wake you, hoping that any moment she would return my call and I would be able to begin. I hope you understand, and there will not be a charge for today. In fact, if you want, we can schedule your next appointment now and I'll take you at your convenience. I do apologize for wasting your time."

"No problem, Dr. Maddox, not a waste of time. Things happen for a reason, and I empathize with that. You were understanding about the traffic, and I understand the situation with the drill," said Linda.

"Thank you, thank you," he was saying under his breath and thinking that it could have been a disaster. *This woman could be dangerous to my health.* "Thank you for understanding. Would you like to come back in a week, say five fifteen?"

"Five fifteen will be fine. I'll be here and on time, I promise. Thanks, Dr. Maddox. You don't know how much I appreciate you."

"No, I appreciate you. See you next week."

"Five fifteen," said Linda as she closed the door, whispering under her breath, "Broken drill my ass!"

Chapter 25

"Hey, girl, told you I'd call you tonight."

"What happened with that son of a bitch?" asked Tasha.

"Not one thing. I mean I wore the sexiest lowest-cut sweater I owned with cleavage showing for days. I had my girls at attention, and he acted as if they were chopped liver. I had thighs hanging out, and I know my stuff is good."

"Did he give you the gas?" asked Tasha.

"Yes, the minimum amount. I could hear him calling my name, I guess to make sure I was not feeling any pain. I instructed him to give me just a little, and he did, so I pretended to be out. I felt if I answered he might give me more. This way if he tried anything I could bust his dumb ass. Now, you know me. That man is fine, and I wished he had tried something. I would have put him in a leg lock and held on for dear life. I knew everything he did, every move he made, and every breath he took. Trust me, he tried nothing, and if he had, I would have told you. Our friendship is more important than anything."

"Damn, I thought we had the bastard. Are you going back? I spoke with Dr. Williams, and she said there was no evidence of rape, forced trauma, or significant bruising or tearing. She also said my hymen could have been broken by sports in high school, college or it could have happened during my childhood. I really don't know. My gut tells me something happened, but I have no choice, and I trust you," said Tasha. "This was a lot to ask, and you are a true friend."

"I'm really sorry, nothing happened. Yes, I'm going back. You know men can't resist me. I always get my man. And maybe he is lying low and is afraid or just being cautious, but time will reveal everything. But a man with a sex addiction will not be able to hide forever. And trust me, he will fuck up one day and fuck me… and sooner than later. Or maybe he's just not attracted to me."

"Girl, please… every man is attracted to you. You have everything a man wants, and your shit is always together," said Tasha.

"I have an appointment next week. In fact, the drill was broken, and the staff had locked up all the other drills. So really it was a waste of time. I wasn't there long, just long enough to let the gas wear off. I'm your girl… I got this. I keep telling you that. Give him time. Do you think he did anything to you the first time you went to him?" asked Linda.

"I don't know. I really don't know."

"Okay, let's give him time to hang himself, and he will with enough time and a long enough rope," said Linda.

"One week from today. I'll keep you posted. How are things going with the braces? Has he tried anything else?"

"Hell no. This is a simple process, and I don't have to be put under. In fact, the whole ordeal takes about ten minutes. I'm safe, but I still want to know. Maybe I'm wrong," said Tasha.

"Maybe you could be," said Linda.

That night, Linda lay in bed, reliving the entire ordeal. Being totally submissive and having to suppress her feelings was the most fantastic experience of her life. She reached three orgasms, expressing herself through controlled moans and a few instinctive quivers. He had taken her to the mountaintop. Reaching over into her bedside stand, she pulled out her mechanical toy and brought herself to another level, thinking only about Harry Maddox.

Chapter 26

It was a cool, balmy morning, and Vincent had been at work two hours when Paris frantically called. She took several deep breaths before saying, "Vincent, oh my god, my water just broke."

"Are you okay? Is the baby okay?"

"Yes, I'm fine, and the baby is too, but I'm not sure how long I have before it comes."

"Honey, it's going to take me an hour to get home, and you should not wait. I thought the baby wasn't due for another two weeks. What happened?"

"Babies don't pay any attention to dates. When they are ready, damn it, they are ready," she said as her voice modulated.

"Hold on. Let me call Sharon… She…"

"I can't wait for Sharon either. I'm calling 911. You and Sharon can meet me at the hospital. Honey, I've got to go," she said as the pain shot through her body.

The ambulance took her to St. Joseph's Hospital. Sharon, Vincent's sister, arrived shortly afterward, and Vincent arrived thirty minutes later. She and Sharon had become the best of friends.

Paris was in delivery, sweating profusely, when Vincent walked into the room. Her pain was almost unbearable, and she wanted the baby out so she could be free. Vincent held her hand as he wiped perspiration from her forehead. "Just hang in there, baby. That little baby of ours is ready to meet its parents."

The doctor said, "It shouldn't be that much longer."

"Get this thing out of me. I don't want it anymore. Just get it out!" shouted Paris.

"Almost, baby, almost," said Vincent trying to calm her.

The doctor and nurses could see she was crowning and close to delivering. "Okay, Mrs. Landry, when we tell you to push, we need you to push as hard as you can."

"Just get this thing out of me now!" she screamed.

"Take a deep breath, and push... push... push," said the doctor. "I see the crown of the head... Just keeping pushing, it's coming." Paris pushed with all her might as Vincent and Sharon watched. "It's a boy. Congratulations! You have a beautiful baby boy," said the doctor.

Paris was exhausted and smiling the best she could as she looked at Vincent. But the look on his and Sharon's faces made her feel ill. She sensed something was terribly wrong with their son. Was he deformed? What type of birth defect could he have? She was terrified and curious but could not see her baby. "What's wrong?" she screamed.

Vincent became instantly pale. The baby began to cry. He looked at Paris and said, "You bitch." Sharon grabbed him by the arm and pushed him forcibly from the delivery room. The doctors and nurses did not know what to say. Dr. Kendall was holding the baby. Paris was afraid. She had no idea why Vincent was so upset and why he called her a bitch. What did she do?

Dr. Kendall laid the baby on Paris's chest and said, "I want you to meet your son."

Paris could not believe what she saw. Her child was not deformed. He was perfect, but he was black. "There must be some mistake. This can't be my baby. This can't be," she kept saying over and over.

"Mrs. Landry, Mrs. Landry, are you all right?" was all Paris heard as the room closed in on her.

"Where am I?" she asked.

"You are in the hospital."

She felt her stomach. "Where is my baby?"

"He's in the nursery."

"Where's my husband?"

"He has not been here since the baby was born."

"What do you mean *since the baby was born*? He was just born. Where is Vincent?"

"Your son was born three days ago," said the nurse.

"Three days ago… What's going on? Will someone just please talk to me," she pleaded.

"The doctor will be in shortly."

Dr. Kendall explained what happened during delivery and that she had gone into shock. He told her Vincent did not want to see her or the baby. Tests confirmed that a black man fathered the child.

"That's impossible. That's impossible. That's impossible… Can I see my baby?" she asked.

Dr. Kendall stayed with Paris as the nurse brought the baby into the room. Paris looked at the child in horror. He was a beautiful baby, but he was not hers. Calmly she said, "This is not my son. What have you done with my son? I want to know!" she began screaming. "What have you done with my son? Get this baby away from me… Give him to his mother and bring me my baby!" she demanded. Holding her hands on her stomach and rocking back and forth, she kept demanding that the nurse bring her baby. She never touched her newborn child again. She was eventually sedated and day by day sank farther and farther into depression, one so deep that returning to reality might not be possible.

Vincent wanted nothing to do with the baby or Paris. She was eventually committed to a mental hospital, declared incompetent, and by default, surrendered her parental rights. Vincent demanded "the boy" be placed into foster care with special provisions. Vincent made a substantial financial contribution to the hospital with an agreement to make annual donations as long as the records indicated that their child was stillborn and cremated immediately after delivery. There was to be no mention of the child's race ever, or the contributions would be discontinued. Vincent filed for divorce on the basis of mental instability.

The story of Paris's mental breakdown and Vincent divorcing her spread through the Valley like wildfire. Dr. Maddox was shocked hearing what happened. He knew how much Paris loved Vincent. Like everyone, he heard the nervous breakdown occurred after the death of their son. He was heartbroken knowing how much she wanted a baby, so her reaction was no huge surprise to him. He had lost a dear patient and at the same time was grateful to have dodged a silver bullet and a wooden stake through the heart.

Vincent hated the thought and sight of the black baby but was much too proud and indoctrinated in his privileged world to let anyone know his wife had been gallivanting around town with a black man. He would rather see the child dead, and to him, he was.

Chapter 27

Maggie, Skyla, and Stephanie tiptoed around the office the entire day, unable to answer one question or do anything correctly. Each was baffled trying to figure out why Harry was so agitated. It was out of character for him to act this way, so to satisfy a question they could not answer, they conjured up the fact that there had been one hell of a fight between him and Katrina. But in reality, it had been one week since Linda, a.k.a. the Black Widow Spider, had been in his chair, and he was so excited about seeing her that it consumed his every reasonable thought and action. Even he surprised himself.

It was five fifteen, and Linda had not arrived. An agitated Harry stood staring out the window like a boy getting ready for his first date. At five twenty, he picked up the phone repeatedly to check and ensure the phone line was not dead. By five thirty he was a complete wreck, sad, disappointed, and feeling totally stupid. Convinced she was not coming, he put away his equipment, pulled off his lab coat, put on his suit coat, turned off the lights, and at five forty-five opened the door. Linda was standing in the door, asking, "Am I too late?"

"No, not at all. Please come in," he said.

"I'm so sorry. I seem to keep getting caught up in traffic. Perhaps I should make earlier appointments to avoid the traffic," she said.

"I promised I would work around your schedule, and I'm a man of my word. It's okay. Please, have a seat in room 2, and I'll be with you in a minute."

Inwardly Linda smiled. She had been watching him from across the street as he stared from the window and purposely waited until he turned off the lights before getting out of her car. She loved the game as much as he. Harry changed back into his lab coat, covering his now-present erection. He slipped a couple of condoms into his pocket and walked into the examination room.

"Dr. Maddox, I'm really so sorry, and I do understand if you can't see me tonight."

"No problem, I was actually putting my time to good use by catching up on paperwork and did not even notice the late hour. Once I realized the time and had not heard from you, I thought you had forgotten or something had come up," said Harry.

Using her seductive voice she said, "I really do apologize. I should have called. I promise to be on time next time."

Linda's attire was killing him. She wore a wrap dress, pair of mules, and her legs were bare. He was thinking, *This is going to be easier than I thought.*

"Let's make the mold of your tooth, and then you can lie back and relax. I know... it doesn't take a lot." He placed the patient bib over her chest, hating to cover them even for a second, and then put the mask over her nose, watching as she relaxed. "Linda." Silence. "Linda," he said, escalating his voice. She was quiet. He loosened the tie on her dress to expose her perfect body only covered by a thong. His penis was hard as a rock to the point of pain. He unbuckled his belt, unzipped and removed his pants. "Linda." No answer. He removed the thong as her mules fell to the floor. "Linda, Linda." She was out, and he was more than ready.

Harry kissed her right foot, and moving slowly up the inside of her legs, he thought he felt her body move under his tongue. He heard her instinctive and familiar moans, increasing his craving. Reaching the top of her thighs the melodious aroma of her sweet spot called his name. He kissed her, feeling compelled to taste her. She moved to his rhythm. Massaging her with his tongue, he continued calling her name, and still no answer. He moved to her stomach and then to her breast, sucking one and then the other. Lost in ecstasy, he rotated between her breast and her sweet spot, sucking and then tasting. She continued to moan lightly as her sounds drove him crazy. The moistness between her legs and the hardened nipples in his mouth turned him into a sex-crazed maniac who could not get enough. His penis was pulsating, and he would not last much longer. Quickly tearing open the condom, he put it on and pushed his hard penis into her warm and inviting cavity. Determined to hold out as long as possible, he moved in and out, up and down, back and forth thrusting harder, then softer, and harder once again. His heart began to beat faster, and his head was spinning. He felt that if he died at this moment, it would have been worth it. Suddenly he exploded. He screamed in ecstasy, and it seemed as if she was methodically squeezing his penis with the muscles inside her vagina. The pain and the agony of pleasure were like an oxymoron, but one he did not want to stop. She was wonderful. She only moaned as he had his pleasure. He pulled out and kissed her wet sweet spot once again.

Harry flushed the condom down the toilet and cleaned himself up. He meticulously cleaned Linda, again to the sound of her sweet moans. He redressed her and, unlike before, began the root canal.

"Okay, Ms. Black, the first stage of the root canal has been completed. I'll insert the temporary crown, and it takes about a month for the permanent crown to arrive. I'll have Maggie call if it comes in before. However, if you have a problem, if it comes off or breaks, call and I will see you immediately. Avoid chewing, especially chewing gum with the temporary. Do you have any questions?"

"No, sir. Maybe one, so I won't come back until the permanent tooth comes in?"

"That's right, not unless you experience pain or it comes off, but if you follow the directions, there should not be a problem. Call me if you have to," he said.

"Thank you. I should be fine. Shall I make the next appointment now? I need a later one… Five-fifteen is perfect, and I promise to be on time."

"Five-fifteen it is. One month from today." *Damn, that might as well be a century*, he thought.

"Hey, this is your girl, Linda. Went to see Dr. Maddox again, and nothing… absolutely nothing. And I know my stuff was tight, I was looking good."

"Well, I'm puzzled. I have not had any problems since that night. When I go to him, he just tightens the braces, and I keep moving. Do you plan to keep going?" asked Tasha.

"Yes, he is a damn good dentist, and you yourself can see what he is doing for you," responded Linda. "But I promise, promise, promise to let you know if he ever gets out of line."

"Okay, girl. Thanks for trying. I guess I was wrong, but thanks for everything. You know you are my real sister. I love you," said Tasha.

"I love you too. See you tomorrow."

Mentally, Harry counted the days, crossing them off one at a time. He checked almost daily to see if Linda's permanent crown had arrived, almost to suspicion. The answer was always "not yet." On day 27 Maggie informed him the crown had arrived.

Feeling like a child waiting for Santa on Christmas Eve, Harry said, "Maggie, please contact Ms. Black and let her know she can take delivery."

"Doc, I've already spoken with Ms. Black. Her appointment is set for Monday at eleven forty-five."

"In the morning?" Harry asked, feeling instantly stupid.

"Yes, eleven forty-five in the morning. Are you taking midnight appointments now, Dr. Maddox?" asked Maggie.

"No, I just thought she wanted something later. She said appointments during the day were difficult. I was simply trying to be customer-driven… that's all," said Harry practically giving himself away.

Harry was so befuddled with the sudden change that he became sick to his stomach. With guilt, fear, and questions going through his mind, he knew it was time to get his practice back on track, vowing never again to see patients after hours. Could Linda know what happened?

On the day of her appointment, Linda arrived looking exquisite. Her every move taunted him, but he was determined to remain focused. He proceeded with caution, waiting for her to drop the bomb any minute. Although he was nervous, the routine procedure was flawless. He handed her a mirror. It was perfect.

"Great job, Dr. Maddox. I think it looks perfect," said Linda.

"I'm glad you're pleased," said Harry.

"Oh, by the way, wondering why I changed my appointment?" asked Linda. Harry was barely able to speak, waiting for the explosion, then Linda said, "Because I had to!"

Harry wondered what that meant. "No problem, I understand." He was afraid of pushing too much.

"You do? And how is that?" she asked.

Feeling as if he were digging himself deeper and deeper into a hole, he was not sure what to say next. "Well, stuff happens. I figured you would return eventually for your permanent crown. The temporary wasn't going to hold up for too much longer."

"See, I was testing your work. Seriously, I'm ready to get back on schedule." She watched the lump form in his throat as he swallowed in slow motion.

"Call and set up an appointment with Maggie. Is this a good time for you?"

She looked at him as if to say *who's playing whom.* "I need an evening appointment."

"My schedule has changed. I'm no longer keeping evening hours. It is too hard on my family."

"That's too bad. I'm so sorry. And I really liked your work. It really has been my pleasure. Thank you, Dr. Maddox," Linda said as she strategically got out of the chair.

"What about the rest of the work we planned?" asked Harry.

"I'll have to find a dentist who can accommodate my schedule. I certainly understand your concern."

Feeling his heart stop and unable to handle the thought of never seeing her again, he quickly lost his newfound conviction. "Well, Ms. Black, perhaps I can make an exception. When would you like to return?"

"What about next Thursday... at... let's say, five thirty?"

"Five thirty it is. I'm looking forward to seeing you."

"The pleasure is all mine, Dr. Maddox. See you then."

Chapter 28

After one year, Natasha was extremely pleased with her smile. Her level of confidence had changed her life, and she could not be happier. She saw remarkable results, but more importantly, no longer feared Dr. Maddox.

Linda's teeth were perfect. She assured Tasha that her dental procedures had been completed, and she was exceptionally satisfied with Dr. Maddox's work. The matter of him touching Natasha inappropriately had become a mute issue.

Linda was going to Harry's office every other week. He would stand in the window, waiting and watching as she arrived. During that time, she toyed and teased him, sometimes arriving late just to make him wait, but never disappointing him. Once, after an extremely fulfilling sexual experience, knowing he was still burning with desire and that he was watching, she deliberately dropped her keys, bent over seductively, dropped them again, bending over even more seductively. Once she got in the car, she pretended to freshen her makeup, observing him in her peripheral vision. She saw his shadowed figure unzip his pants, retrieve his penis, and jack off. He was so deep into the moment that he did not notice her watching. She observed until his body quivered with pleasure, smiled, and then drove away.

Linda was always eager to see Harry and loved every moment with him. She enjoyed the way the nitrous oxide knocked off the edge, providing a feeling of euphoria. She no longer played the game of making him wait. She had fallen in love with a man who thought he was the only one receiving pleasure. He scheduled her late enough to avoid the staff, and she was rarely billed for services.

He had replaced or redone everything in her mouth possible, sometimes repeating procedures to ensure they were perfect.

It had become Harry's routine to watch for her, loving her every catlike movement. She had a seductive, smooth, and graceful way of getting out of her car that only she could do, and she wore almost nothing. As she approached the door, he would step back and let her ring the bell twice. She knew his routine as well. "Good evening, Ms. Black."

"Good evening, Dr. Maddox," said Linda.

"Please, how many times do I have to ask you to call me Linda? Ms. Black is so formal. Why are we still so formal? It's Linda."

"Okay, Linda it is." This reminded him of the time Paris requested he call her Paris.

"What are we doing today, or shall I ask, what are you redoing?" she asked.

Harry did not know how to respond. Her appointments had become routine, and he realized she never asked what was next. She just showed up and gave him free will over her mouth. "Well, Linda, we are just about through with your procedures. I don't think there is much I can do, except pull your teeth one tooth at a time."

They both laughed. "Thanks, but no thanks." She realized their run was coming to an end, and she had to do something.

"Let's get started, Ms. Black... I mean Linda."

She knew the routine. She sat in the chair as he laid her all the way back. She smiled as he placed the mask over her face. Her eyes followed him. He could feel the excitement. He watched as she became more and more relaxed. She looked so peaceful. He removed the patient bib, calling her name, and as normal, there was no response. He untied the all-familiar wrap-style dress exposing her thong. "Linda, Linda, can you hear me?" he asked. Nothing. He could hear her breathing, and it appeared to be deep. She was relaxed. He lowered the chair, lifted her body to remove her dress and thong, leaving on her high heels. He knew every part of her body, having had her more times than he could count. He felt his penis harden. It was always the same.

He kissed the top of her feet, moving up her calf to the inner thigh. He called out to her softly, "Linda… can you hear me? I wish you could hear me." And staying true to form, she did not respond, except with her all familiar moans from his very familiar touch. He reached between her legs, massaging and kissing her soft sweet spot. She moved gently. He continued to move up her body, kissing her abdomen, then her breast. He kissed her neck reminding him of the first time he ejaculated licking her clean. Kissing her on her neck, she moved slightly. "Linda." She did not respond. He moved back to her breast, kissing them, sucking them, and manipulating her nipples with his tongue until they became firm. Again, he kissed her between the legs, tasting her, and she was sweet. He could feel her move and hear her moans. He couldn't stop because she had become his poison. He rotated between her breast and her sweet spot. It felt good; she felt good. It was driving him out of his mind. He manipulated her breast, then her sweet spot. He had one breast in his mouth and his hand between her legs massaging her, feeling her warmth with his finger, in and out, in and out, caressing her breast with his tongue, sucking harder and harder. She could no longer hold it in and screamed with pleasure, her body reacting to the greatest and most powerful orgasm of her life.

Harry froze, scared shitless. He was busted, and his career was finished. He could not move, because Linda had become the aggressor. "Don't stop, please don't stop… Yes, that feels so good… just don't stop. Come on and fuck me. Oh yeah, that's right, oh yes, right there, yes… oh yes… oh my god… Oh, don't stop… Please, yes." She looked at him and said, "My mother always said, if you're gonna get screwed, you might as well get the sugar." A somewhat perplexed Harry was incapable of caring. She took control simply by talking to him, pulling him into her, flesh to flesh. He thrust his penis into her, harder and harder, back and forth, up and down, until they climaxed simultaneously. She said things most women would not, exciting him even more. She kissed him passionately, and he returned the kiss, reaching up to turn off the nitrous oxide. He held her tightly on the tiny chair, too weak to move. She was everything he wanted in a lover.

Harry stood up and put on his lab coat and apologized. "I'm so sorry. I don't know what got into me. You were so beautiful, and I just couldn't control myself. This is the first time anything like this has ever happened. I am so sorry. Please, can we talk about this?"

"Dr. Maddox, save that bullshit for somebody else. I think I'll call you Harry. This is not your first, second, or third time. You can't even count the number of times you've... enjoyed my body."

Shocked, he could not speak.

"It's okay. I let you make love... or I should say take advantage of my body, no wait... really nonconsensual sex is actually rape. Man... you were driving my ass freaking wild. I was about to blow my mind. You were not the only one getting off all this time. I could win the fucking Oscar Award for pretending. Being in this chair was hard as hell. I would leave here, go home, play with my toys, and scream my fucking head off... I could feel your tongue all over my body, tasting me, kissing me, sucking my breast, and driving me crazy. You're fantastic and knew exactly what to do."

"I... I don't know what to say."

"There's nothing to say. No apologies needed. I knew every time you performed a procedure and the many times you only screwed me. Oh, you did something all right."

"But I'm so sorry. This is..."

Linda stared at his fantastic body, remembering how great it felt next to hers. She sat on the end of the chair, one knee swinging from side to side and the other opened approximately forty-five degrees. She was in no rush, knowing he enjoyed looking at her. She continued talking, not certain if he felt uncomfortable or not. She said, "Hey, Harry, where's the warm wet towel? It always felt sooo good when you wiped between my legs, so gentle and caring... come on and finish the job. Oh, Harry, the time you really turned me on was the time you licked your cum from my breast. See, I remember everything."

Harry's turned beet red. He was speechless.

Using her sexiest and most sensuous voice, she said, "What's wrong, Doc? Cat got your tongue? Nope, you don't use that tongue like a cat... without a tongue." As she stood, Harry could appreciate the total perfection of her nude body. Not only were her breasts perfect but also her ass. She walked across the room, wearing only heels, tormenting him. She bent over and picked up the towel, wet it, and handed it to him, saying, "Finish the job." She walked back to the chair, laid back, parted her legs, and said, "I'm all yours, I'm waiting… Finish the job."

Harry wanted to tear into her, make love and never let go, but the pain in his loins was making it impossible to stand straight. It felt like his life was moving in slow motion, and he had no idea what to do next. He was having an out-of-body experience, frozen in time.

Linda wanted him as well but realized she was right where she liked it—being in control.

"On second thought, Doc…" said Linda as she took the towel from him. "It's getting late." She wiped herself suggestively and dropped it to the floor. Turning her back to him, she located her thong, bent over, and put them in her purse. She picked up her dress, slipped it on, tying it at the waist. Taking out her comb, she restyled her hair, put on lipstick, and picked up her purse. Every movement she made was deliberate, calculated, and seductive. Looking back, she said to him, "I guess we need to reschedule my appointment… didn't get around to finishing that last job. Oh, I'm sure there is no charge for today's services. I'll reschedule… Expect my call." Linda walked over to Harry and took his face in her hands kissing him passionately. He grabbed her waist, pulling her into him. She taunted him, pulling away, and as she did, the tie of her dress loosened, exposing her body. He pulled her to him, kissing her gently on the lips, her neck, and her breast, slowly working his way to the navel. She leaned back in his arms as if she was a contortionist. For the first time, they engaged in consensual sex, a session that lasted until nine that evening.

Chapter 29

The next three weeks were hell for Harry. Linda played with his mind. He could not sleep, eat, function, or predict her next move. She had not called and literally had him by the proverbial balls. He tried imagining what she might do or if she might broadcast it to the world. Since she was never completely under, she was a willing participant, but no one would believe him. He was afraid, but her mystery constantly intrigued and excited him. He wanted to talk to her and tell her how sorry he was for everything. He wanted to tell her just how important she had become to him.

At five fifteen, three weeks later, Linda called, and a nervous Harry answered the phone, "Hello."

"Hi, Harry... got time to see me today? My tooth hurts."

"I was on my way home. Katrina and I have plans for dinner... and..."

"Cancel them... I have a dental emergency, and I need you to fix me. The pain that's raging inside is so intense, and I need relief," Linda said seductively melting his heart.

Harry was afraid to say no, and her voice excited him. He needed to know how she felt and did not want to jeopardize his chances of never seeing her again. At this moment, it was evident she had the upper hand. "Okay, I'll call and delay our plans. What time can I expect you?"

"Look out your window, unlock the door, then call and make your excuses."

When Harry opened the door, Linda had already untied the bow, revealing her nude body. Locking and bolting it, he watched her walk toward examination room 3, dropping her dress to the floor, and his urge to take her became overwhelming. He stepped over it and wrapped his arms around her from behind as she pushed her naked body into his. She moved seductively from side to side, pressing her buttocks harder and harder into his crotch. He kissed her neck, and she could barely breathe. She turned around, grabbing and stroking him as they melted into the moment. "Whoa… back up, Doc. Have you forgotten to call the wife? Don't want anything to disturb the mood."

"Oh yes… yes, you're right. Give me a moment." A fully clothed and nervous Harry walked into his office, but a completely naked and perfectly sculptured man returned, one Linda could not help but admire.

They caressed each other, synching their bodies to the rhythm of the moment. She touched his body from head to toe, examining and kissing passionately every inch of him from top to bottom. No woman had ever made love to him or his body as she was doing, so unselfishly, giving him the gift of her love and pleasing him beyond expectation. He exploded without penetration. After resting, Harry initiated the second round of foreplay, knowing he had not satisfied her. Suddenly he stopped. "What's wrong?" she asked.

"I know this may sound crazy, but I… I want to ask a favor…"

"Okay, what is it?"

"Do you mind if I give you a little nitrous oxide?"

Linda looked at him strangely and asked, "Why?"

"It's just the way it's always been, and I was always in control. It intensifies the mood… and… drives me crazy. The gentle moaning makes me want to scream."

"You do realize I was pretending to be under? The moans were for real… Hey, it's okay. I like the way it makes me feel. It gives me a great high, makes me feel powerless. I could make love to you either way. Whatever makes you happy. Remember, just a little… this time I am a full participant."

He was surprised but thrilled she agreed and placed the mask over her nose. He caressed her breast in his mouth as she moaned to his delight, but this time, her moans were not subdued.

Linda told Harry she believed she was infertile. She wanted a baby badly for the wrong reason. She wanted someone she could love the way she had never been loved and someone who would love her. The sex was the best either of them had experienced, and they threw caution to the wind having unprotected sex. Linda's desire for a child overshadowed her sense of reasoning. Her determination to get pregnant and deal with the consequences later was a chance she was willing to take.

Harry shortened his office hours on Thursday with his last appointment at one. He informed his staff he would use the afternoon to complete paperwork. They were dismissed at three, and he continued to compensate them for the hours not worked. Linda became his weekly Thursday afternoon and evening appointment, and of course, at no charge.

Linda clearly understood the boundaries of their relationship and embraced their "no commitment" and "absence really does make the heart grow fonder" attitude. She loved the excitement of their secret romance, toying with his mind when seeing him in public, especially when he was with Katrina. She never complained or placed demands on him. He watched her every deliberate move. She loved the tease, knowing she would pay for her misdeeds on the following Thursday. The sex was rougher yet more passionate, and her punishment was receiving enough nitrous oxide to be completely submissive.

Chapter 30

Until Linda met Harry, she and David Mann had been in an exclusive relationship for over five years. He was kind, lavished her with gifts, took her on exciting and expensive trips, but could not compare sexually to Harry.

Harry treated her well and, out of guilt, paid for several trips she and her great friend took. He had no idea it was Natasha. He would be ruined professionally if he left his family for a woman like Linda. His daughters had grown into beautiful young ladies and were doing well academically and socially. He was indebted to Katrina for always having his back, but he had fallen in love with the seductive and adventurous nature of Linda.

Harry sensed a woman as sexually fluent as Linda had to have another man, maybe even two, but the less he knew, the better. She deserved to be taken out, wined, dined, and shown off, something he could never do. Linda had given him a key to her condo, but he understood the terms of usage. She never invited David to affairs where Harry might be, nor did she mention him. The terms and boundaries she established were enough to satisfy his male ego and provide just enough hope to make him believe he was her only man.

Chapter 31

Natasha trusted Linda emphatically, and she had proven to be a true friend. Secretly Natasha was grateful to have been wrong about Harry. He had given her a beautiful smile, the one thing she needed to feel completely confident and comfortable. They were closer than sisters, sharing everything. Within Bethel Industries, Natasha was advancing quickly, and it was rumored that she was in line to replace Mr. O'Malley as vice president of marketing upon his retirement. She was ready for the honor and the opportunity to make history.

She attributed her confident smile to meeting Ken at a company outing eleven months earlier. He was ten years her senior and lived in San Diego. He had never married, did not have children, and until meeting Tasha, considered himself a confirmed bachelor. He treated her with the utmost respect. On the night he proposed, they shared a passionate night of intimacy. He was gentle, tender, and everything she expected the man to whom she gave her virginity to be.

She thanked God she waited.

Despite Linda and Natasha's similarities, they were from different worlds. In spite of loving each other unconditionally, Linda knew that Tasha could never accept her relationship with Harry. She had already betrayed her trust by crossing the line. Before moving to Montgomery Valley, men had always controlled her life. She was sincerely sorry knowing she allowed a man to destroy what they had. However, the last thing she wanted was to annihilate Harry, and if the truth were known, his career would be over. Natasha was raised in the streets, but it was the brutal streets that raised Linda, and there was a defined and significant difference between the two.

Chapter 32

For the last ten years, the Montgomery Valley Country Club, Bethel Industries, LLC, and the city cohosted its annual New Year's Eve celebration gala, with the chairmanship rotating annually. It was Bethel's turn to serve as the lead host. To be invited practically authenticated one's place in the Who's Who of the Valley's Social Registry. Natasha planned to publically present Ken to her boss and coworkers as her fiancé. Linda invited David as her escort, especially on New Year's Eve. The large ballroom accommodated three dance floors. Three newly installed screens were lowered from the ceiling, and each was strategically positioned to allow those seated in the rear to experience a panoramic view. Natasha and Linda were seated at separate tables near the front.

Harry and Katrina had been added to the guest list for the first time. They were seated near a large monitor, permitting a clear view of everything. As cameras spanned the room, Harry was surprised to see Linda, and she was elegant. Unable to remove his eyes from the screen, he watched for every opportunity to glance at her, wondering whose guest she was. Harry heard an inaudible announcement being made. He could see the screen clearly but had to listen carefully to understand what was being said. Linda was standing in the middle of the room as a man knelt on one knee. What the hell was happening? Observing carefully, he saw the man take the microphone. Harry could barely breathe. Miraculously, he clearly heard the words, "Linda, the love of my life, you are the most beautiful woman in my world. You are my princess, my love, and my heart. I am asking you in front of all these witnesses if you would do me the honor of being my wife."

Linda appeared genuinely surprised as he opened a box containing a beautiful three-carat solid round-cut diamond ring surrounded by a band of smaller diamonds. As the cameras focused in on the crowd, everyone could be heard gasping for breath. Linda was stunned. She did not hesitate and said, "Yes, yes, David, I would love to marry you." She and David embraced in a passionate kiss as Harry bent over in pain, and the room exploded with thunderous applause.

The staff congratulated the couple on their engagement, including Natasha. Harry's face froze, and time stood still. Katrina noticed his blank stare and asked what was wrong. He shrugged her off. Unable to move, he continued to stare at the screen. He almost fell out of his seat when he watched Linda and Natasha embrace and then engage in a lengthy conversation. An uncomfortable level of fear set in as he wondered how long and how well they knew each other. He tried convincing himself he was reading too much into the situation, but the feeling in his gut told him otherwise.

Harry wanted to tuck his tail between his legs and run, but he was more interested in figuring out their relationship. Katrina tried engaging Harry in conversation, even asking him to dance, and he did, but the tone of the entire evening had changed, and she had no idea why.

Prior to midnight, the president of Bethel Industries made a champagne toast. "Good evening... Good evening, good evening. I want to say thank you to each of you. We have so much to be thankful for. We are a family, and each time we celebrate an engagement, wedding, or a birth, our family grows. Tonight we have been particularly blessed. One engagement I was aware of, but Ms. Black's engagement came as a complete surprise. I am pleased and honored to announce the engagement of our very own Ms. Natasha Campbell to Mr. Kenneth Crater. I feel like the proud father of these two beautiful and dynamic women. I want to say congratulations to Linda and David and to Natasha and Kenneth. May you have long-lasting and successful marriages." As the spotlight moved to reveal both couples, Harry's heart stopped in his chest. His lower jaw dropped, and he felt light-headed. "Good luck and may you be blessed in all your future endeavors. Okay, everyone, we are close to the hour we have waited for. It's time to lift your glasses high. Ten, nine, eight, seven, six, five, four, three, two, one... Happy New Year!"

Chapter 33

On Thursday immediately following the New Year's Eve party, Linda arrived at Harry's office, finding the atmosphere cold and clammy. She reached out to hug him, but he blocked her embrace, grabbing her left hand. "Where's your engagement ring?" he asked in a demanding tone.

"Engagement ring?" she asked.

"Don't play with me, Linda. I was there and heard the announcement. You are nothing… nothing but…" said Harry.

"Nothing but what? What are you trying to say? You… you a married man, with two children. What are you trying to say about me? I don't have… I don't have the right to have a life. A man who can take me out, someone I can be seen with in public, someone I can be with without hiding in a dentist office, being screwed in a damn dentist chair or a brief booty call when you can break away. What are you trying to say? I really can't believe you!"

"Linda, it's just that I love you so much. You mean so much to me. You are my life."

"Yeah, sure, but Katrina is your wife!"

Harry began to cry, something he did not think he was capable of doing. He had been in control for so long, but her engagement knocked him for a loop. "I have not been able to sleep. I can't fathom the thought of you being with someone else."

"Harry, come on now. You have a wife, and I had to have someone. His name is David, David Mann, and he is special to me. I love him, but I'm in love with you. He is someone I can have, be with, and share a life with. You are someone I cannot have. I love you so very much, but I can't have you. We can't go out, not to dinner, to the movies, not even to a hotel. You made that clear from the beginning. I accepted it. I've never asked you to make a choice. I have always known that I didn't have a claim on you. There is absolutely no future for us. What more do you want from me?" asked Linda.

"I can't live without you, and I can't live with the thought of someone else having you."

"Harry, listen to what you are saying. Just listen to yourself. Did you really think you were the only man in my life? It's something we never talked about, but you knew there had to be someone. You can't live without me? How about telling that to your dear precious wife? You can't live without me. Who do you think I am? Yes, Harry, I love you too, but... are you going to leave Katrina and marry me?"

"Honey, it's not about Katrina right now. It's about Beverly and Angela. This is just not the right time. I know the time will come, but now is not that time! Just be patient with me. I promise I will work everything out. And yes... a part of me hoped I was the only man in your life. I never asked because I knew the truth would hurt, but just not this much. I thought I'd let sleeping dogs lie and just be happy pretending to be blind to my beliefs. Linda, you know how I feel about you."

"And how is that?" she asked as she pulled him close, wiggling her body into his. She could feel his manhood rise as she kissed him passionately. She had regained control.

Linda and Harry became closer, professing their love to one another as they had never done before. Neither of them talked about Katrina or David. She began wearing her engagement ring, taking it off just before making love to Harry. He refused to look at it. Harry asked her about her relationship with Natasha, but she convinced him that they were merely acquaintances, assuring him that Ms. Campbell was much too far up the corporate level to associate with someone of her secretarial status. Harry heard and believed what he wanted.

Chapter 34

Linda was eagerly helping Tasha plan her wedding, but each time Tasha asked Linda about hers, Linda would remind her that one wedding was all she could handle at a time.

Linda began experiencing severe headaches, reminding her of the sporadic episodes she had as a child. They seemed to dissipate after leaving the slums of Boston. Her family lacked the financial resources to cover the costly CAT scans, MRIs, and other costly tests doctors wanted to perform. Her coping method was to retreat to a quiet dark room and lie still until the pain subsided, and for the most part, it worked. As an adult, Linda followed the same practice. Tasha, worried about her, repeatedly encouraging her to go to the doctor. She promised to make an appointment but never managed to follow through.

Linda had a reoccurring dream about her wedding. She was the beautiful bride wearing a white silk and lace gown studded with pearls and crystals. Her veil was approximately ten feet long and lingered behind her as she walked the 250-foot rose-petal-covered aisle of the church. She walked slowly, deliberately, allowing the guests to take in her full beauty. The gown fit her body perfectly as it should, after all, it was a one of a kind and designed for her, made to fit her body, and she had spent a small fortune on it. The church was packed to capacity. She chose not to be escorted down the aisle because she had never had a father figure in her life and thought it would be pretentious to have someone play father of the bride on the biggest day of her life. Cameras were flashing all around. She was the most photographed bride in all of Montgomery Valley. This was the happiest day of her life. Nothing could be more perfect. She was excited, feeling beautiful inside and out. She strolled carefully and strategically down the aisle, with each step bringing her closer to the love of her life. And when she reached the altar and turned to look into the eyes of her groom, it was never David; it was always Harry.

Although the engagement was unexpected, Linda was impressed at how well-thought-out and beautiful the proposal was and felt compelled to say yes. She knew the moment he asked that she would never marry him. She felt it was time that Harry saw her with David and hoped that he would become insanely jealous. She determined who would be invited to this New Year's Eve gala, planned Harry and Katrina's attendance, sent the invitation, and recorded the RSVP. Harry's reaction was exactly what she hoped for, but even she could not have written a better script.

Chapter 35

Harry and Linda spent significantly more and more time together. A few months later, Linda, tired and feeling used, threatened to go public. Livid, Harry begged her not to betray him. He started taking her to selected medical conventions, especially the ones in Hawaii and on weekend excursions, but for a woman like Linda, he had to do more. He did more, but it was just not enough. Oftentimes, after making love, violent arguments occurred. Her demands became greater, and he wanted nothing more than to please her. She kept putting pressure on him, and finally, he agreed to leave Katrina, explaining it would take some time to work out the details. If Katrina found out, after killing him, she would use this as ammunition against him. His greatest concern was disrupting the lives of his daughters.

Four months later, after making love and during one of their many routine arguments, Linda lost her balance, almost falling. Harry caught her, noticing she felt cold and clammy. He laid her on the chair, asking if she was okay. The room was spinning, and her sight was slightly blurred. Linda appeared confused, frightened, and barely able to focus. "Harry, I don't know what's wrong with me. Can you take me to the hospital?"

They were naked, and Harry had to think fast. "Baby, let's get you dressed first. Let me help." It took him over fifteen minutes to put on her clothes. Her body appeared heavier than normal, like dead weight, and that was frightening. He then put on his clothes and took a few deep breaths to compose himself.

"Listen, baby, I'm going to put a cold wet towel on your forehead. Just lie still for a minute. You should feel better soon. Maybe you just need oxygen," said a confused and unsure Harry. How could he explain taking her to the hospital so late or calling EMS? Someone might talk. "Let me drive you home. I'm sure you'll feel better after getting some rest. You're just tired, that's all."

"I don't know… I feel confused, crazy, like something is really wrong. It's strange. I really want to go to the hospital. My vision is a little blurry. I don't think I can drive."

"Trust me, you'll be all right. I'll take you home and stay with you until you go to sleep. I will get your car to your home before daybreak. And if you can't sleep, I'll call EMS and have them pick you up at your place."

When Linda's alarm sounded at five o'clock the following morning, she was alone and scared. She did not hear Harry leave, nor did he wake her to say good-bye. Still slightly disoriented, she tried standing, and it was difficult keeping her balance. It was too early to call Harry. She dialed the wrong number three times before reaching Tasha, who immediately instructed her to call EMS. "I'll meet you at the hospital," said Tasha.

Linda underwent a battery of tests, CAT scans, MRIs, neuro- logical exams, and X-rays. Tasha was there when Dr. Franklin, the head neurologist, came with the results. Linda held Tasha's hand tight, sensing the news was not positive.

"Ms. Black, I'm Dr. Franklin. How are you feeling?"

"I don't know. Why don't you tell me?" she asked.

"Hello, I'm Dr. Franklin," he said extending his hand to Natasha. "Are you family?"

"Yes, she is," stated Linda. "Anything you say to me, you can say in front of her. In fact, she is my next of kin and will handle all medical decisions related to me, if I am unable to do so." Tasha was surprised with that revelation but loved Linda as a sister and would always be there to support her.

"The scan shows that you have a tumor on the left side of your brain."

Unable to speak, tears streamed down Linda's face, and Tasha felt numb. She was on the verge of tears but knew she had to remain strong. They would get through this together no matter what.

"What does that mean? Just take it out!" she said in a demanding voice. "You can take the damn thing out, can't you?" she asked.

"We hope so. We will run additional tests and biopsy the tumor to determine if it's benign or malignant. We have scheduled a biopsy for six thirty in the morning. The procedure should take about two hours. Allow me to explain what we will do. We'll drill a small hole on the left side of your skull just above the tumor and snip a small piece to be biopsied. We should have the preliminary results within twenty-four to forty-eight hours."

Linda did not hear one word after *biopsy*. Tasha listened carefully, and it took a few moments before realizing the seriousness of the situation. "Linda, get some rest. I'm going to work. I need to arrange and rearrange a few meetings, but I will be back later to stay with you tonight. I'll be here when the procedure is done. I promise I'll be with you through everything. Don't worry, I promise everything will be just fine. If you need me, I am only a phone call away."

"Tasha… am I going to die?"

Shocked, she looked at Linda and said, "No, you have too much to live for. After all, you have to help me finish planning my wedding. You are my maid of honor, and without you, there will be no wedding. And remember, I am your maid or matron of honor whenever you set that wedding date. You're not cheating me out of that opportunity. Have you called David?"

Linda shook her head negatively. "I'll call him. You go to work. See you later, and I love you, girl."

"Okay, baby, love you too!"

Chapter 36

Natasha kept her word, returning to the hospital with her overnight bag. Linda was happy to see her. David had been there and wanted to stay, but they agreed she would be fine with Natasha watching over her, and he promised to come back in the morning.

"Tasha, do you think I am going to die?"

"Linda, I think you'll be fine. We have to wait on the results and remain positive. Remember, God is in control. You can't worry right now, that's too hard. We just have to wait, sweetie."

Tasha and Linda spent the rest of the evening and into the night reminiscing about their lives as friends and the good times they have shared. They talked about the day they met, what thoughts each had about the other, their commonalities, their men, challenges, trips, shopping excursions, families, every single thing except her relationship with Harry, eventually drifting off to sleep.

At five o'clock, the nurses came into the room to prepare Linda for surgery. She had barely slept, waking up throughout the night, wondering if the tumor was going to be malignant or benign. An eerie feeling of discomfort nagged at her. Tasha sat quietly in the corner of the room with her knees folded to her chest, rocking back and forth, praying and worrying, struggling not to show fear while trying to remain positive. As Linda was rolled from the room, Tasha kissed her and said, "I love you, girl. Everything will be okay, and I'll see you in recovery." David arrived just in time to see Linda. He gave her a kiss of encouragement and told her he loved her.

Linda was not into the religious thing. She felt life had treated her unfairly and that she was not on God's priority list. Heartbroken, shocked, scared, and unsure of her future, she felt God did not believe in her. As she was wheeled into the operating room, she began to pray. For the second time in her life, she asked God to help save her life. She needed something, a faith she rarely relied on or believed in.

Linda was in surgery for three and one-half hours. The procedure was more complicated than anticipated because of the placement of the tumor. They were trying to bypass the optic nerve and avoid the possibility of causing blindness in the left eye. Eventually, the doctors were able to clip a portion of the tumor.

While in recovery, Dr. Franklin met with Natasha and David. "I am concerned that the results might not be favorable. The tumor has been growing for quite some time. There is a strong possibility it is malignant. Even if it isn't, because of the location, if removed, it might render her blind or in a vegetative state for the rest of her life." Their hearts skipped a beat as they grabbed each other's hands, holding tight for support.

"What are we supposed to do?" asked Tasha.

"If you believe in prayer, I suggest you pray. However, until we know for sure, I encourage you to remain positive and supportive. And should the results not be what we hope for, she will need your support more than ever," said Dr. Franklin. "The nurses will let you know when you can see her."

In silence, Natasha and David returned to the waiting room and waited to see Linda, wondering what they would say. They greeted her with a smile. "Hey, baby," said David.

"Hi, girlfriend," said Tasha.

Groggy and struggling to speak, she asked, "Is it over? What did the doctor say?" asked Linda.

"They extracted a piece of the tumor and sent it to pathology and will have the preliminary results in a couple of days," said Tasha. "But right now, you need to get some rest and stop worrying."

"Am I dying? That's really all I want to know," asked Linda.

"Girl, you have to think positive and—" said Tasha before being cut off by Linda.

"Don't bullshit the bull shitter. I know I'm dying. We're all going to die... Hell, we were born to die. If we were all born to die, then why the hell were we ever born? Nothing makes any damn sense at this point. I'm okay. Thanks for being here."

"We're not going anywhere. We'll be right here," said David.

Still struggling to speak, Linda said, "No, I want you both to leave. I need some time to myself. Just give me a minute. I know you haven't eaten. Go get something to eat, and I'll see you in a few."

They looked at the nurse who nodded in agreement. Each gave her a kiss. "We'll see you in a few, kiddo," said Tasha.

Chapter 37

Tasha and David spent most of the day in silence as Linda slept. They knew there was nothing they could do, but felt comfortable being there to keep an eye on her. It had been a long day, and they decided to leave at five. Linda was relieved. She watched and waited long enough to be sure that neither doubled back and then picked up the phone and called Harry.

Unable to recognize her voice in the beginning, Harry was speechless about what he heard. So many things went through his mind. She could have died in his presence; he should have taken her to the hospital instead of taking her home, or he should have called EMS. He did all the wrong things. Feeling bad for the way he handled the situation, he wanted to run to the hospital and be by her side, but she was not his wife and he had to practice caution.

Harry arrived at seven that evening, wondering what he would say if he ran into anyone he knew. When he reached the room, Linda was excited and waiting for his embrace, but he remained distant.

Somewhat lethargic, she asked, "What's wrong? No hug?"

"This… this is not the time or place. We have to be discreet. I don't want anything to jeopardize the divorce."

She was disappointed, but hearing him say he was still planning to divorce made his action tolerable, and a hug was not worth endangering that. Harry had just given her the major reason she needed to beat this damn brain tumor.

"How long will you have to be in here?" he asked.

"I don't know," she said smiling. "The doctor said it could take up to forty-eight hours to get the results. Waiting is hell… that's the worst part… waiting. I don't know if it's malignant or benign or even if they can remove the damn thing."

"I'm sorry, baby."

"So am I," said Linda.

"Look, you'd better get some rest. I'll call you in the morning and check on you. Love you," said Harry as he left.

Linda watched him exit after less than ten minutes. She felt empty, wanting him to stay, to hold her, give her a kiss, caress her, rather than treat her as a casual friend. She craved for at least a kiss on the cheek, but he merely squeezed her hand and left. Her anger and hurt were overridden by his declaration of divorce.

Chapter 38

Two days later, Dr. Franklin received the results of the biopsy and did not look forward to delivering the news. He was glad Linda was not alone. "Hello, Ms. Black."

Staring directly at Dr. Franklin, Linda said, "Just spit it out." She grabbed Tasha's hand so tight it cut off her circulation. "Just give it to me straight, Dr. Franklin."

"Ms. Black, the good news is that the tumor is benign, but… because of the location of the tumor, it is inoperable. It is a rare, extremely slow-growing tumor that has probably been growing since childhood. There should have been symptoms such as headaches or blackouts. If we could have gotten to it years earlier, we may have been able to remove it, but… something has caused an acceleration in its growth. Perhaps some type of chemical… something you have been exposed to repeatedly. It's really hard to say, but if you're careful, you can live another three to five years, possibly longer. But you do have to be careful. You could undergo radiation to shrink it, but this is a weird tumor, and the radiation may have the opposite effect, causing it to grow. You are the only one who can make that decision. We'll continue to run tests to see if we can determine what may have caused the growth acceleration. Because of the location and the length of time you have had it, it has integrated itself into the brain." Linda was heartbroken.

Tears filled Tasha's eyes and ran down her face. She wanted to go somewhere and scream but could not leave Linda, not now.

"What quality of life will I have?" asked Linda. "Will I be a vegetable?"

"No, not at all... You can live a good life, but there will be limitations. As it grows, your headaches will increase over time. If we attempt to remove the tumor, then we definitely run the risk of you possibly not recovering, and the chances are about 95 percent that if you do, you could enter a vegetative state. You will eventually become blind in the left eye as the tumor puts added pressure on the optic nerve. Eventually, you will not be able to drive because of seizures, and you may not be able to work full-time once the headaches increase, but you can work for as long as you feel healthy and are able to do so. We need to make sure that whatever accelerated the growth is not something you are exposed to at work or come in contact with regularly."

"Oh god, what am I going to do?" asked Linda.

"I'll be here for you. You don't have to worry about anything. I'll be here," said Tasha.

"I know, I know..." said Linda.

"And I know David will be here," said Tasha.

Linda thought to herself, *David is the last person I want to spend my dying years with, a man I do not love.*

"You will have to let us know if you want to try radiation," said Dr. Franklin.

"Dag, that's messed up. If I do the radiation, will I be bald?"

"No... more than likely you will not lose your hair," he said.

"God... why didn't I just die?" she said.

"Ms. Black, I don't know if you believe in God, but if you do, turn to Him. He has given you a second chance in life, even if it is only three to five years. Take the opportunity to enjoy the time you have left. This is man's diagnosis. God has not spoken, not yet," said Dr. Franklin.

Tears flowed freely as Linda and Tasha embraced. Tasha thanked the doctor, and two hours passed before the two exchanged another word.

Chapter 39

"Tasha, I couldn't ask for a better friend. You are great and have been with me through this entire thing, through everything. Please go home and get some rest. You need it, and I need to be by myself."

"Are you sure?" asked Tasha.

"Yes. Plus, if I kill you while you are taking care of me, then what good are you to me?" said Linda smiling. It was the first time either of them had smiled in days.

Linda sat quietly, trying to determine her feelings. Was it anger about the tumor? Was she angry with Harry, angry with God for giving it to her, or angry that the secret she was holding inside might have been the catalyst that accelerated its growth?

Her life changed in such a short period, but it seemed like a lifetime ago. She was in and out of depression, hating Harry one moment and missing him the next. His position in society did not allow him to freely visit her in the hospital. She was exhausted, so much to digest. She prayed for peace, finally falling asleep, and slept the best she had in four days.

It was six in the morning when Linda felt a presence in her room. Opening her eyes, she saw Harry standing beside her bed. "Hi," he said. Linda blinked several times to make sure her eyes were not playing tricks on her. He pushed a bouquet of flowers in her direction, saying, "These are for you."

"Is this a peace offering?" Raising her voice, she asked, "Where in the hell have you been? I thought you were going to call!"

"Look, baby…"

"Look baby my ass. Please don't! I'm too tired. No excuses please… no more excuses."

"But I would have—" he said.

Linda interrupted him, raising her voice, and once again said, "Please... Harry, I said no more excuses." Lowering her voice, she said, "Do me a favor... just leave. And take your little peace offering with you."

"Please, Linda... Please listen. I'm so ashamed of myself... the way I have acted."

"You should be!"

"I'm not going to offer excuses. I just want to say I'm sorry and didn't mean to hurt you I... couldn't stand the pain of seeing you this way. It just... it just hurts so badly... and I am so sorry," he said as he cried.

Although her heart went out to him, she was not going to have any of it. After all, she is the one dying. "Yes... yes, you are. You are one sorry son of a bitch, and I'm sorry I ever met you!"

Harry stood at attention, hurt and surprised by her reaction. He sat the flowers on the stand beside her bed and called her name. "Linda... Linda." She did not respond, turning her head in the opposite direction. Turning slowly, he lowered his head and walked to the door.

Stopping and turning back to face her, he said, "I love you, baby... I really do. Good-bye."

He watched as she knocked the flowers to the floor, and when he turned to leave, he was staring directly into Tasha's face. Embarrassed, he lowered his eyes to the floor and quickly acknowledged her presence only by nodding as he rushed past her.

"What was he doing here?" asked Tasha sternly.

Linda turned around, surprised to see her so early. "He's my dentist... remember?"

"Yes, he's also my dentist, but he'd never come to visit me in the hospital unless I was in a car accident and my teeth were knocked out. Your teeth are perfect." Looking around, she asked, "What is this mess all over the floor? What happened with the flowers?" Cleaning up, Tasha continued, "Plus, I'd never want that man to come visit me. I still think he's not right. I don't trust him. I'm grateful to him, but I really don't like him. How did he know you were here? What's going on?"

"I could ask you the same thing. You are giving me the third degree. Okay, Counselor, am I on trial? That's something I don't need right now. The last thing I need is for you to come down on me."

"Linda, I'm not coming down on you. I have only one question—did he ever try anything with you?" she asked.

"No, now let's just drop it. I'm sick and tired of you asking me that. I thought we dropped that subject a long time ago. If you came here to bitch at me, then please leave. Why are you here so early anyway?" asked Linda.

"I couldn't sleep, so I decided to come check on my girl. Is that okay?" asked a shocked Tasha. "I'm sorry, I did not mean to upset you." Tasha felt embarrassed, and the last thing Linda needed was to be upset.

They sat for the next three hours with hardly a word spoken between them, each examining their feelings. Linda was wondering if her lie backfired. How much did she hear Harry say? How long had she been standing at the door? Tasha wondered if Linda had lied to her. Was there something she was not telling her? Harry was never mentioned again.

Harry left the hospital more nervous than when he entered. He had no idea that they were close friends. Linda said they were acquaintances, but acquaintances do not show up at six thirty in the morning. He always suspected that Natasha did not trust him, but they had developed a respectable relationship. How long had they really known each other, and how close were they? How much did Natasha hear? Did she know of their relationship? He was worried sick but scared shitless to call Linda. She was so angry, and he had to be careful. All he could do was pray, wait it out, and hope she would call.

Chapter 40

David and Tasha were at the hospital to take Linda home. Linda wanted to talk about her plans for the future, work, and how she would spend the time she had left. They tried to convince her to think positively, not about dying but about living. David wanted to get married immediately. Tasha wanted to travel. David wanted to move in and take care of her. Natasha said she would take a couple weeks off and help Linda get situated. David wanted to go to the justice of the peace and only have Tasha and Ken as witnesses. Tasha wanted to plan a small intimate wedding where they could have pictures to remember the day. The room was spinning, and Linda said, "Stop, you guys! Give me a chance to plan my own life, and it might not include either one of you." Then she broke out in a hardy laugh and said, "Just kidding. I love you both, but I do need some time to internalize this mess. My life is predictable, and my days are numbered. I know I'm dying, and until I do, I'll plan how I'll live the rest of my days."

After David left, Linda told Tasha she had no intension of marrying him. Although he was a good and kind person and his proposal was beautiful and touching, she could not embarrass him publically by saying no. She admitted she was once deeply in love with him, but not anymore and could not spend the rest of the life she has left making his life miserable.

Linda rested on and off as Tasha worked around the house, cleaning and dusting. She was disappointed at Linda's revelation about David. She liked him and wanted Linda to have the comfort of a special male presence to help her through this ordeal. At midnight,

Tasha decided to leave but was willing to stay if Linda wanted. "I'll be just fine. You have already done so much," said Linda.

Tasha tucked Linda into bed and kissed her on the forehead, "I'll see you in the morning. Love you... and sleep well," said Tasha.

"Good night, and thanks again for everything... but most of all for being my friend."

Linda was wide awake by six the following morning. She waited until six thirty to call Harry, knowing he was in route to his office. He saw her number on his caller ID, and the rhythm of his heart sped up. He answered, "Hello."

"Hi, Harry," she said.

"What's going on? How are you... are you okay? I'm pleased but surprised to hear from you again," he said with a tone of confusion, anger, and excitement.

"Why do you sound so angry?" asked Linda.

"And how am I supposed to sound? What am I supposed to feel? I must ask you, how long have you known Ms. Campbell? How do you know her?" he asked demandingly.

"Our offices are next to one another," she said calmly.

"What? So you lied to me?" he said.

"How did I lie to you?"

"Look... I'm almost at the office, and I have to go, but we need to talk. Soon!"

"Good... What are you doing for lunch? Why don't you come over?" she asked.

"I'll be there at twelve fifteen. Will you be alone, or do I need to bring lunch for three?" he said sarcastically.

"Two... only two, and I'll—" She heard the phone click in her ear without him saying good-bye.

Linda needed time to pull herself together. Immediately she got up and went into her bathroom. She found a nice scarf to cover and disguise the bandage around her head. She dressed in a sexy nightgown with a matching robe, put on makeup, and waited. She knew her attitude had been erratic and did not know what to expect.

Harry used his key to unlock the door. She instantly saw the anger on his face. Walking over to him, she tried calming him down with a hug, but he stepped back. She began to cry, something Harry had never seen her do.

"Harry, I have three, maybe five years to live. I don't want to live like this. I want to be happy. Spend the rest of my life with you."

Harry was stunned. "What are you saying?"

"It's simple. I want to live the rest of my life with you, open and not hiding. I want to be your wife. You were planning to leave Katrina anyway. You'll just have to expedite the process."

"What do you mean I'll have to expedite the process? How can I… What do you expect me to do?" he asked angrily.

"What? You said you were going to… divorce Katrina. You have got to stop jerking me around," she said in a demanding tone.

Linda talked to him about her relationship with Natasha, explaining that she was an executive who was quickly moving up the corporate ladder and that she coordinated meetings between high-powered executives, which included Ms. Campbell. Again, she assured him that their relationship had always been professional but her illness brought them closer. She told him everything the doctor said. His guilt grew, suspecting the accelerated growth might be related to the repeated use of nitrous oxide. She insisted he divorce immediately or pay the price. They both knew this was one argument sex would not resolve. Harry became so angry, ripping the key from his chain and throwing it at her saying, "I've had it, Linda. No more threats and no more of your damn demands. Do whatever it is you have to do. I'm out of here. I've tried to tell you over and over that now is not the time. My daughters are in a position that a divorce would tear them to pieces. How could I face them? What would I say to them? Yes, I love you, but I need to keep my family intact just a little longer. How can I trace around town with you on my arm?" Catching himself, he continued, "What I mean is that I just can't break up my family right now and chance destroying their lives. Linda, baby, I love you, but just do whatever it is you have to do!"

He slammed the door as he left, hoping she loved him enough not to betray him. Now Harry had regained control. Linda was vulnerable, dumfounded, and uncomfortable.

Chapter 41

Linda cried for the next two weeks. Harry did not call, and she refused to call him. She made a personal vow to somehow, someway get even, but spreading news of their affair around town would only make her the villain and the Valley whore. In addition, she could not admit to Tasha she lied.

After two months of recovery, Linda returned to work. Bethel Industries allowed her flexibility in her hours. She went back full-time with the ability to leave early if she felt tired. She had been a valuable asset to the company and was given an assistant making her return easier.

She was in an out of depression and wanted Harry in her life and in her bed. She and Tasha would go shopping and to lunch, but it was not enough to pull her out of depression. She finally told David she did not love him enough to marry him and it would be unfair to do so at this stage in her life. She attempted to return the engagement ring, but he refused to take it. She told him he deserved better than she, and the last thing she said as he left was that she would see him at her funeral. Tasha continued to plan their European vacation, but Linda was busy planning her funeral.

Six additional months passed, and Linda had not seen or talked to Harry, but thought about him daily. There was still a void. Harry missed her in spite of her actions, lies, and threats. He loved and appreciated her for not following through with her threat of broadcasting their relationship. Her illness forced him to refocus on his personal and professional life, hoping it was not too late to repair his marriage. He had not touched a patient since Linda and no longer scheduled appointments without the presence of a staff member, no exceptions.

Eight and one-half months after their last encounter, he recognized her number. He fought not to answer, but she was his addiction. He felt he was approaching the finish line of his recovery process, and accepting this call would sabotage forward movement. Cautiously he answered, "Hello."

"Hi, Harry, it's good to hear your voice. You sound good."

"So do you," and he meant that with every fiber of his body.

"I'm so sorry we fought. I was wrong trying to force you into a divorce. I had no right. I'm dying, and… I was unfair. No one wants anyone that they know is dying. Please forgive me."

"Linda, you don't have to say these things… it's okay."

"I want you to know I'll always love you and—"

"Where's this coming from?" said Harry as he cut her off.

"From my heart. Out of my love. I was irresponsible and feeling sorry for myself. I was having my own pity party. It took me this long to realize misery really does love company. I thought about it, I have a second chance. There's time left, and I still have a lot of living to do. When I die, I'm going out in a blaze of glory. The entire world will know that Linda Black lived and lived her life the way she wanted and that she is gone but not easily forgotten."

"I'm glad to hear you sounding so positive and know that I will never forget you. This is the Linda I know and the one I love and the one I will spend the rest of my life loving."

"Yes, baby, I'm back. Harry, let me come see you. I have a tooth that was damaged when I was hospitalized. It needs to be checked and possibly repaired. How about five thirty this evening?"

"I've cleaned up my act, baby. I don't do evening appointments anymore. You were my last evening appointment."

Sounding rather sexy and alluring, she said, "Can't you make just one little itty-bitty exception, just this once? I promise not to ever bother you again after this. I promise, baby, on my Girl Scout's honor."

Never able to resist her, he said, "You've never been a bother. Come on in. I can't wait to see you. And you were probably never a Girl Scout."

"Maybe, maybe not. See you later… and you know I'll be on time."

Chapter 42

Harry hurried through his appointments finishing ahead of schedule, making sure his staff could leave without delay. In the meantime, Linda spent the next three hours getting ready, curling her hair, soaking in a milk bath, and giving herself a mini pedicure and manicure. She put on the diamond stud earrings and diamond drop necklace Harry had given her one year as a Christmas gift. She found the red stilettos with the ankle straps that drove him wild. She had not determined which wrap dress she would wear. She stood in the full-length mirror, admiring the way she looked, thanking God for her close-to-perfect figure. She was extremely pleased with her body, checking herself out from every angle. Her legs were shapely, and there was no cellulite. Her stomach was firm, free from stretch marks because she had never given birth. Her breasts were firm, still standing at attention, and she wondered how any man could resist all of this. When she felt pleased with the way she looked, she slipped on a light trench coat, grabbed her purse, an envelope from the table, car keys, and headed to the garage. She felt strange, liberated, and free for the first time in months. She had one stop, and that was to mail the envelope she held in her hand.

Linda pulled up to Harry's office and sat in her car, taking a few deep breaths in an attempt to relax. Harry watched as she drove up and wondered if she was okay. All the suppressed feeling he once had, all the hurt, the anger seemed to float out the window as she approached the door. He could feel himself becoming erect and could not wait to greet her. He lunged out when opening the door. "Whoa, big boy… what's the rush?" asked Linda.

"I've missed you so much baby, and you look so good. It's been too long. God, how I've missed you," said Harry.

"I've missed you too, and you look even better to me. Why don't you get the stuff ready?" asked Linda.

"I don't think so. I don't want to use anything that'll hurt you. I can't do that."

She was surprised, and for one brief moment, she thought he meant it. "Please, just a little… I promise this will be the last time. I deserve to be totally submissive because I was a very, very bad girl. I want you to take me any way you want."

This request aroused Harry to the point that he could not say no. "We really don't need it. All we need is each other," said Harry.

"I know, but just this once," she said dropping her trench coat to the floor. All she was wearing were the red stilettos, a diamond necklace, and diamond earrings. Shocked by the unexpected surprise, he became putty under her control. He would have done anything she asked.

"Okay, baby, just this one last time, and I mean it. Don't ever ask me to do this again!"

"I won't, and that I promise. Just allow me to indulge in my fantasy this one last time. I love you so very much."

"And I love you too," he said turning on the nitrous oxide.

Harry was completely under her spell. "Okay, baby, whatever you want. Just promise me you will never leave me again." He watched her walk through the office like a gazelle, smooth, lean, and elegant. She was truly a beautiful and seductive woman. He missed her, her spunk and sassy ways. She walked to the edge of the chair and sat down, legs parted, inviting him to take her. She taunted him by fondling her breasts. Then she stuck her hand between her legs, bringing out one finger and sticking it in her month. He was mesmerized. She put her hand back between her legs, once again bringing out one finger, this time sticking it in his mouth. He was like a sex-crazed wild man. His erection was hard and painful. She unzipped his pants, and they fell to the floor. He removed his boxers, maneuvering them over his erected penis. She kept taunting him, licking her lips and then kissing his penis lightly. She stroked and kissed him simultaneously. He was losing control, remembering how much he missed her.

Suddenly she stopped and said, "You need to get comfortable. Go pull off the rest of your clothes and put on one of the lab coats that I have grown so accustomed to. I'll be right here waiting. Oh, and don't forget to take your pants."

She admired his statuesque body as Harry reached down, picked up his clothes, and went into his office. He was strikingly handsome, and his body was the best she had seen, and she had seen many. Linda quickly grabbed a rubber glove and placed it under her body. Then combed her hair and freshened her makeup. She wanted to look her best. It did not take long for him to return. She was driving him crazy with desire and jealousy.

"Baby, you know I don't want anyone else to have you. I want you to be mine and mine alone," said Harry.

"I called off the engagement with David right after my hospitalization. You are my only love, and I can't share myself with anyone other than you. You belong to me as well. Till death we do part."

"Well, baby, I am yours. Katrina and I tried to make a go of it over these months, but it's just not there. You are my heart, and I love you to death."

He was saying all the right things. Maybe this was the day he would commit to her. "Are you leaving her? Are we getting married?"

"One day, baby, one day soon, I promise. I just have to wait to get the girls through this crucial stage. Angela is in college, and Beverly will graduate next June. Once Beverly is in college, my life will be straight."

Her dreams were short-lived. He just messed up the mood and said the wrong thing. She was tired of the words *not now*. "Wrong answer, baby. I'll probably be dead before she finishes high school."

"Shh! Don't talk like that. You know you are going to pull through this. Just think positive," said Harry.

"I love you, and I promise we will be together one day soon, either in heaven or hell," said Linda.

Being in the heat of the moment, Harry heard what she said but did not understand what she meant. However, he did not want to spend precious time figuring it out because his penis was ready to take the plunge. They would have plenty of time to talk about it later; now was the time to make love and not war. It had been far too long.

Chapter 43

Harry turned on the nitrous oxide, taking precautions to give her a very small amount. He carefully mixed a higher concentration of oxygen to a lower amount of nitrous oxide, basically administering oxygen only. While he waited for her to relax, he fondled her breast, sucking them gently, first one and then the other, slowly then rapidly, slowing down and starting over. Gently, then harder, it was driving Linda wild. She enjoyed the tenderness of his touch and the aggressiveness that followed. He gently massaged the moist spot between her legs and then climbed on top of her, gently penetrating her with his deliberate and smooth method, in and out, in and out, pushing himself into her just a little farther with each inward stroke. He could hear her moans, and he loved the sound. He began to match her moans as the sounds escalated to pure ecstasy. For the first time in over a year, they reached an orgasm simultaneously. It was more fantastic than either of them remembered.

"Oh god, it's been so long. I'm so sorry." She felt him move as he began to get up, but she held him close. "No, please... don't move. Your body feels so good next to mine."

Harry, feeling the same, said, "I've missed you so much. I didn't realize how much until now. I could stay inside of you forever."

He felt her body demanding more and responded, stroking her, in and out, up and down, each fighting back the urge to explode. Linda watched the movement of his body, taking it all in. They looked into each other's eyes as their hearts beat in rhythm until exploding simultaneously. Harry, completely spent, did not notice Linda reach beneath her body, slip the rubber glove onto her left hand, and adjust the controls, turning the nitrous oxide to its highest level and the oxygen to the off position. She managed to remove the glove and dropped it in the trash can she placed next to the chair.

"Harry… Harry," said Linda as she nudged him. "I really do love you. In spite of our differences, our ups and downs, the things we've been through and the things we have yet to face, I love you."

"I love you too," said Harry.

"Hush, I'm not through, you have to let me finish! You hurt me, but that's all right. They say every dog has its day." Speaking quickly, she continued, "You broke your promise, lied, and when I got sick, you were nowhere to be found… and still I loved you. I tried, but I couldn't stop loving you. You told me several times you were going to divorce Katrina and marry me, but you had no intention of doing that. Yes, I loved David at one time and that man loved me, but I broke his heart when I told him that I did not love him enough to marry him. I told him he deserved better than me. And he does. I hope that someone finds her way into his heart and loves him for the good man he is. I chose to spend my last days loving you, and my god, I loved you. You were the reason I fought to live and the reason for which I am willing to die. When you are deep in your grave, know that I love you because I will take this broken love with me to my grave." It sounded as if she was slurring her words, but he knew it was the nitrous oxide.

Harry was perplexed but continued to lie on top of her, wondering where this was coming from. He was not sure what to say and decided to say nothing out of fear. After noticing a significant lull, Harry thought it might be safe to speak. "Where is this coming from? I'm sorry. I was wrong, and I accept that, but I want to make it up to you. I don't want us to argue again, not ever. I miss you with every breath in my body. I've tried to stop thinking about you and tried fixing my marriage by pretending you never existed, but it's been tough. Baby, I don't want to live without you. I don't care about time or what I may have to give up. I'm telling Katrina tonight that it's over and I'm leaving. The girls will be fine, I'll see to that. We will never be separated again, I promise you that. Baby, I love you, and I'll make it all up to you. I feel so badly about the way I've treated you, and I'm so ashamed. I promise… I promise I'll make it up to you."

Suddenly Harry felt Linda's arm drop lifeless to her side. He jumped to his feet, looking at the nitrous oxide level and realizing it was at its highest. How could he have made such a mistake? He was sure he checked it. Unable to think clearly, he turned it off and performed CPR. He felt for a pulse, but it was extremely weak. He began crying profusely as he frantically tried to figure out what to do next. He dressed himself, cleaned her up, and looked for her clothes. He gave up looking and administered CPR once again. He turned on the oxygen and continued to search the area for her dress before remembering the only thing she was wearing was a trench coat. Scared shitless, he had no choice but to put it on and button it. He removed the earrings and necklace for fear that it might be traced back to him if she did not pull through. How could he explain any of this to anyone?

With Linda still on oxygen, he cleaned the area around the chair to eliminate the possibility of anyone finding semen or other incriminating evidence. He was certain there would be an investigation and questions like, why was she here at this hour and why was she only wearing a trench coat? What was he supposed to do? Should he put her in her car and push the car over a cliff into a river. They didn't use a rubber, so his semen was going to be present. His DNA was going to be all over her body, and he was simply screwed. He wiped every part of her with antibacterial soap and then gathered the trash and towels, placing them in the can beside the chair. He took the bag from the wastebasket and put it in the trunk of his car to dispose in a location far away from the office.

Desperate and knowing he would be the prime suspect, he began to pray. He did not know how he would explain to EMS, the police, or his family why a woman would ever be in his office completely nude. He thought about putting one of his lab coats on her, but that was a sure giveaway because his name was on every coat. He wanted to save her but wanted to save himself more. He gathered her belongings, put her in her car, and drove five miles away to a cheap sleazy motel where the atmosphere was dark and dingy. He parked in the lot and checked to see if his presence might be visible from a motel window. Believing he was safe, he transferred her to the driver's side, making sure the doors were unlocked. He hoped the authorities would think she was with some lowlife putting an end to a long and drawn-out investigation, lessening the probability that she would be tested for semen. He checked her pulse, and it was weaker than before. He prayed for her recovery; however, in his heart he believed she was already gone. Harry pulled the collar of his coat up around his face, put on his fedora, and walked into the dark dingy lobby of the hotel, screaming, "There's a woman is a car in the lot. It looks like she's dead. Call the police, quick!"

The desk clerk quickly picked up the phone and dialed 911. When he looked up to speak with Harry, he was gone.

Linda was rushed to the emergency room and placed on life support.

Chapter 44

As Natasha retired for bed and sat down to read a book, her phone rang. At first she was sure it was Linda, but her caller ID indicated it was the hospital.

"Hello."

"Ms. Campbell?"

"Yes, this is she."

"This is St. John's Hospital. Ms. Linda Black has listed you as her next of kin."

"Yes?"

"Can you come to the emergency room immediately?"

"I'm on my way, but what happened?"

"Dr. Franklin will speak with you when you arrive."

Natasha hung up the phone without saying good-bye and quickly threw on some clothes. She wondered what could have happened? Was Linda all right? Was she in a car accident? She told herself to just stop worrying and concentrate on getting to the hospital safe and sound. She wondered why Linda did not call her first. Closing out all negative thoughts, she wanted to believe Linda was fine.

Dr. Franklin was waiting. "I'd like to speak with you first." She followed him into the ICU as she looked at Linda through the window. "Ms. Black's living will designates you to speak on her behalf. Unfortunately, she sustained considerable brain damage." Tasha gasped for breath. "I know this is hard for you, it's hard for me, but no matter how many times this happens, it never gets easier." Dr. Franklin handed her a box of tissue. "We need your permission to remove Ms. Black from life support. There is no brain activity, and she is, for all intents and purposes, brain-dead."

"What happened, Dr. Franklin? I thought she had more time. She didn't seem to be that close to the end. I saw her this morning, and she was fine. I don't understand what happened," said Natasha.

"I can't answer that. She was brought in by EMS approximately two hours ago. By law, an autopsy is required once she expires. She was found in the parking lot of that motel, the McLemore on the west side. We will know more following the results of an autopsy," said Dr. Franklin.

"Why, why would she be on the west side, especially at some dirty cheap motel? This is not like her. May I see her, please? God, I'm not ready for this. I'm really not ready for this. This is just too soon!"

Dr. Franklin escorted her into the room and squeezed her hand gently before leaving. With tears streaming down her face, she took Linda's hand in hers. "Tell me why. What happened? Speak to me, damn it! Why were you at some two-bit lowlife motel? Why? Talk to me, please! What was going on? I trusted you with my life. I love you like a sister. You were my closest and dearest friend, and I would have done anything for you. I wish there was some way I could have helped. Why didn't you just talk to me? I'm not ready to give you up, Linda. I can't... not now. Saying good-bye is the hardest thing I've ever had to do. I love you, I love you... my sweet friend." She placed Linda's hand across her chest and sat next to her lifeless body until one o'clock in the morning. Dr. Franklin had seen this type of thing many times, but it was never easy. He remained patient as he waited for Natasha to make the call. "Please disconnect her. She is already gone. And I want a thorough autopsy performed! I mean it, and I'll pay for it! I need to know exactly what killed her."

Linda lived one hour after being disconnected, and Tasha was at her side. She talked to her, hoping that something she said might have gotten through. When Linda flatlined, Tasha called for the nurse. She kissed her friend on the forehead and said, "I know some-how, someway we will find out what happened." Tasha left without ever looking back.

Chapter 45

Unable to sleep, Harry tossed and turned, feeling as if the world were closing in around him. He got up early, specifically to watch the morning news as the story of Linda's death hit the airways. "Young executive secretary found near death in the parking lot of the McLemore Motel on the west side, later dies after being taken off life support. Details when we return in three minutes." Harry was devastated and doubled over in pain. The last he checked, she was in critical condition, but he hoped for a miracle and that she would pull through. He promised God that if she did, he would stand beside her this time. "Now back to our top story... Ms. Linda Black, a fifteen-year resident of Montgomery Valley and executive secretary of Bethel Industries, LLC, was found near death in her car in the parking lot of the McLemore Motel on the west side. Ms. Black was wearing only a trench coat and a pair of red high-heeled shoes. Her ID and purse were found in the car, so robbery does not appear to be the motive. The business card of a prominent local dentist was found in her coat pocket. His name is not being released because he is not believed to have been involved. The motel clerk could not identify the male who reported seeing Ms. Black and requested he call the police. The clerk stated that the man did not remain at the scene. He is reported to be a black man, about six feet tall, with a slender build. It is possible he may have played a part in Ms. Black's demise. A hospital spokesperson said Ms. Black was brain-dead upon arrival and placed on life support. Approximately nine months earlier, she was diagnosed with an inoperable and slow-growing brain tumor but was given an encouraging prognosis of three to five years and possibly longer according to Dr. Franklin, the attending physician. An autopsy has been requested to determine the actual cause of death and if rape may be a factor in this case. Additional details will be given as this story develops. Stay tuned to Channel 5 for the latest in your local news."

"A what?" Harry asked himself. "Who in the hell ordered an autopsy? God I hope they won't question me. Why the hell did she have my card in her pocket? I never thought to check her pockets. Why would I? What are they looking for by doing an autopsy?" He threw up in the middle of the floor.

Chapter 46

Early on Monday morning, Tasha called Bethel Industries, officially informing them of Linda's death and requesting time off to handle her affairs. She was preparing for a ten o'clock appointment with the funeral home when the phone rang. "Hello, Ms. Campbell, this is Dr. Franklin. I have the preliminary results from the autopsy."

"Hello, Dr. Franklin. Thank you for calling. What did they find?"

"It appeared she died from a toxic overdose of nitrous oxide. We also found fresh semen, indicating she had sex prior to being brought to the hospital."

"Sex... sex, she had sex!" Calming down, she asked, "Do you think she was raped?"

"No, there was no sign of forced trauma, tears, or bruises often-times indicating rape. It appears to have been consensual."

"So it was not the brain tumor... nor was it just a routine procedure that killed her?" she asked.

"Remember, this was only the preliminary exam. The final results will take weeks. These tests are still inconclusive. We need to be certain there were no other drugs in her system, which may have reacted with the nitrous oxide, causing the brain damage or her death. The question we need answered is why such a high dosage was administered? Too much can cause irreparable damage to the brain and nervous system, or it can kill, which appears to be the case with Ms. Black. When the autopsy is complete, her dentist will more than likely be questioned, but that's a matter for the police."

Good, she thought. She did not even ask who the dentist was because she did not have to. She knew. Her mind was racing as she said to herself, *I know that bastard's responsible, and somehow and in some way, he's going to pay, if it's the last thing I do.*

"Ms. Campbell, Ms. Campbell, are you still there?" He was sensing he had lost her.

"Yes, I'm so sorry. My mind drifted. Please let me know when the final results are in, and thank you so much."

"I'll call you as soon as I hear from pathology."

"Thank you, Dr. Franklin. Thank you."

Tasha cried like a baby. "Why didn't you talk to me? Tell me why? You could have talked to me about anything. We were best friends. I would not have judged you." Hearing the results made it harder to do what had to be done.

Exhausted, she struggled through the ordeal of the morning, making arrangements, picking out what Linda would wear, and deciding on a location and date for the service. She needed to lie down. When she closed her door, an indescribable emptiness came over her. With tears blinding her, she stumbled over a pile of mail that had fallen from table. She wanted to kick everything to the side, but needing a distraction, she picked it up and decided to sort through it. She almost passed out when finding a letter from Linda. She staggered to a chair and sat down to catch her breath before opening it.

Dear Tasha,

If you are reading this, it means I have died. My life has been in danger for the past few months, and the man responsible is Dr. Harry James Maddox. Please go to my condo, and you will find a letter hidden under the nightstand on the right side of my bed. It will explain everything, the lies, threats, and deceit.

I hate to involve you, but you are the only one I can trust. I know best friends are supposed to talk about everything, but it is because of our friendship that I decided not to endanger your life. I am telling you now because a man is guilty of murder, and he should never walk free. I am afraid of him and what he is capable of doing. This letter is my ace in the hole and something you will understand later.

Know that I love you and am asking your forgiveness in advance for putting you in this position. Your sister always.

Love,
Linda

Visibly upset, she stuffed the letter in her purse and drove cautiously to Linda's. Using her key, she slowly opened the door and turned on the light. Walking into the condo gave her a very eerie feeling. She felt as if something or someone was holding her back, but she was on a mission that overrode her fear. She found a package exactly where Linda said it would be. Sitting on the edge of the bed, she tore into a large white envelope. Enclosed were two letters, one addressed to Natasha with "Confidential—read me first" written on it, and the other was simply addressed to Natasha. She opened the one with "Confidential" written on it.

Chapter 47

My dearest Tasha,

You are my dearest and closest friend, the only true friend I've ever had. I did not deserve your friendship, and I am sorry for any and everything I may have done to betray you or cause you pain. I betrayed your trust, but never meant to hurt you. You know by now that I've not been honest about my relationship with Harry. I know you have suspected that since seeing him at the hospital.

You were right. Harry is a sleaze ball, a womanizer, and everything you said. I'm sure he took advantage of you even though he never admitted it. I'm sure he is guilty of everything you suspected. I know what he is capable of because he did everything to me.

More hurt than surprised and with tears running down her face, she continued reading.

I am so very, very sorry, but I thought it was different between Harry and me. I thought he loved me, and a part of me really thinks he did. He told me I was the first woman he had ever gotten involved with. I found him mesmerizing from the first moment I saw him.

He promised to leave his wife, and I believed that lie. He was kinky, an excellent lover, and we deserved each other. Neither of us was any good. He was the first man, other than David, who treated me like I was someone special; he was different from anyone I had ever met. I liked the freaky things we got involved in. He made love to every inch of my body. I have done some terrible things in my life, but betraying you was the lowest. I was afraid if I told you the truth, you would have exposed him, and his life would be over. And selfishly, the life I had come to enjoy would have died as well.

Tasha, I am begging you not to judge me for the life I have lived. I did the best I knew how. I have always had the propensity to fall for the wrong men. This time was no different. Harry and I argued constantly about his off-and-on divorce, but I obviously loved him a lot more than he loved me.

What angered and bothered me the most was his insistence that we use gas every time we made love. I hated it and was afraid it could cause some type of long-term damage. I asked him repeatedly if it was safe, and he assured me it was. I loved him and trusted him not to do anything that would hurt me. I was shocked and disappointed when I found out the growth of my brain tumor was accelerated by the constant use of what he called "the stuff." When I confronted him, he said he was sorry but was not responsible because I wanted it too. He had given me megadoses without considering what might happen, slowly killing me, but he did not care as long as he got off. He said the more he gave me, the more he was in control.

Tasha, I have been completely honest with you this time. I wish I could make him pay. I know what I am about to ask takes nerve, but I really need your help and hope you will not fail me as I have failed you.

I understand this entire thing is hard to believe. I did not set out to hurt you or betray your trust. I felt that if you were not involved in our relationship, your conscience would be clean. I started out trying to help you, but my selfish desires got in the way. I have to avenge my death. Why should he go free for what he has done to me, to you, and who knows how many other women? I am certain we were not the only ones he has sexually assaulted, actually raped, in that damn dentist chair. He has to be stopped before he kills someone else. I failed you in life, but I can help you in death. What happened to you will never have to come into the light. You will be safe. We can get him, if you still want to. If so, you must destroy this letter and then read the second one. If you choose not to help, I will understand, but you must destroy all three letters and let the courts run its course. There will be a trial, and his patients will be called to testify.

Had I lived, I planned to intercept your mail, sparing us both. If he had kept his end of the bargain, I would have spent the rest of my short life doing all of the things I wanted to do, as Mrs. Harry James Maddox, and… with my best friend of course. Take that European trip for both of us.

When I moved to Montgomery Valley, it was for my safety. I left my past behind. My mother's name is Katherine Black, and she lives at 33579 S. Hogan Street. Her phone number is

555-786-9987. She is really a beautiful woman who simply had a very difficult time finding her path in life. I should have been a better daughter by staying in touch, but I was afraid she would be in danger by knowing where I was. I told you about Horse, and he never gave up looking for me. He felt he owned me and not in a good way. Please find her and tell her that I love her and that there was not one day that I did not think about her and my sisters, Melissa and Gail.

If you are willing to help, put the third letter into the envelope you received in the mail with the postmark and take it to the police. Remember, girl, I love you, and one day, if God forgives me, I will see you in heaven, and if not, I will see Harry in hell!

Love,
Linda

Tasha felt as if she had been blindsided by a Mack truck. She did not know what to do but was too involved to stop now. Curiosity compelled her to read the second letter.

Dear Tasha,

If you are reading this letter, it is because I am no longer alive and my death must be investigated. I hate to burden you, but I do not know whom else I can trust to get this into the hands of the proper authorities. I have been afraid for my life for quite some time. The person out to kill me is Dr. Harry James Maddox. His practices are unethical and demeaning, especially to his female patients. The contents of this letter are going to be difficult, but must be known. He has to be stopped.

I became one of his patients almost three years ago. What was supposed to be a routine cleaning, minor dental work, and a root canal became a one-man orgy. He insisted on giving me nitrous oxide on every visit. I asked if this was necessary, but he said he would give me just a little to relax me and help with my fear of dentist. I later found out it was only necessary for root canals and difficult procedures. He always scheduled my appointments when his staff was not present, saying that was his only availability. In the beginning it was great, not to have to take off time from work, but it seemed that he would never finish, and it took a lot of my personal time. I requested earlier appointments. He said his schedule was booked, and since he was so close to completing the work, it would be easier to leave me where I was.

Almost a year ago, during a root canal, I had the strangest dream. It felt like I was having sex. I could feel hands all over my body, but I was in a fog, half awake and half asleep. It was strange. I felt my body quiver, and I thought I was having a wet dream. This is embarrassing, but it has to be said. I opened my eyes and realized I was not dreaming. Dr. Maddox was on top of me. his eyes were closed as he moaned and groaned, reacting to his obvious orgasm. I could not move. I was powerless. The mask was still over my nose, and my level of consciousness was not completely clear. I seemed to be drifting between a twilight stage and unconscious stage. I still believed it was a nightmare. He began to raise and lower his body, pushing himself into me and did not stop until he ejaculated again. I was powerless to speak or raise my hands to push him away. I could not remove the mask because my hands would not do what my mind was telling them to do. I felt powerless. Although I could not move, I could only yell out, but my screams were silent. The tears ran down my face. This man was literally raping me. This was not consensual sex. He was raping me, and I could not do anything but surrender under his power. I hated him.

When he realized I was awake, he looked at me and smiled. He got up, stepped back, and began straightening his clothes and zipping up his pants as if he had done nothing wrong. I could not believe his nerve. I was sick, disgusted, ashamed, embarrassed, scared, and afraid to take my eyes off him.

Once the gas wore off and out of fear, I could not speak. I cried, and he said nasty things, blaming me, saying, "Pretty girls have to be responsible for their own actions." He threw me a towel and told me to clean myself up. He said if I decided to talk, it would be my word against his, and no decent person in this community was going to believe a whore like me over a respected professional of the community. He said I brought this on myself by the way I dressed, but I am a human being who can dress any way I desire. Regardless of what a woman wears, no one has the right to take advantage of her. He is a rapist… convicted or not.

I was afraid to return to his office and afraid to go to the police. When I became ill and the neurologist informed me my tumor was aggravated by an overexposure to some type of chemical, I began retracing my steps. I thought about where I had been and what I may have been exposed to. I remembered the nitrous oxide and began researching its effects. I have experienced so many of the symptoms, such as tingling sensations in my legs, feet, and hands. I had no idea what was wrong. I suffered from what is known as "behavioral disinhibition." Big word, isn't it? He was slowly killing me. Prolonged use of nitrous oxide can damage bone marrow and the nervous system. With this new information, I confronted him by telephone, and he denied responsibility. I asked him how he could explain all the visits and I do not remember anything. I threatened to go to the police, the newspapers, and the American Dental Association. He begged me not to, saying he wanted to talk. He asked if I had discussed what happened with anyone else. I was truthful and told him no. That was purely out of embarrassment. He begged me to keep it between us until we talked, asking if we could meet in private.

There were many phone conversations to discuss the repercussions this could have on his career and family, but when I asked how he felt about the repercussions the nitrous oxide had on me, he became agitated. This man is directly responsible for my death. He said he would call later but demanded I keep silent and he would make it worth my while. He went on to say that in the long run I would be the one hurt, that he knew people in high places who could make my type look very bad. He said there were a dozen men who would say that they had slept with me. How can a person make up for killing someone, cutting his or her life short? I asked how often he had taken advantage of others, but I could hear the smile in his voice, and he refused to answer. Can this man be believed?

Three days ago, Dr. Maddox called, saying he wanted to make my life memorable. I asked how even though I did not trust him. I asked if he could make the tumor go away and give me my life back. He said no; however, he could make the time I have left comfortable financially as long as I kept my mouth closed permanently. My flesh curdled at the way he said it. He asked to meet in his office on Friday to discuss the details. That's two days from today. I asked why there, and he said it was the only place which would not draw suspicion.

My gut, that tiny voice inside of me, kept telling me he could not be trusted. I am not sure what to do. Should I press charges and take him to court, and if I do, I could spend the rest of my life fighting, which is not living. It is not important what happens to me because I am already dead. If he compensates me while I am living, then I will listen. I will demand he never touch another patient or I will go to the police, and I told him that. If I don't do this, I will die anyway, and he will continue to do what he has always done, and he knows I will be here to watch him like a hawk. What is he going to do to me, kill me? I'm sorry, he has already done that. He asked me to take a taxi, but I am going to drive, just because I can. Maybe he does not want any evidence. Just kidding, girlfriend.

As your BFF, I am begging you to forgive me for not sharing this with you. It was embarrassing, humiliating, and something that was very hard to do. I did not want to endanger your life. Since I am dead and will not be able to talk to the police, please let this letter written in my handwriting speak for me.

You are my friend in life and in death.

I love you,
Linda

Tasha became angry, choking on her own hatred. Struggling to breathe, and her dislike for Dr. Maddox and everything he stood for escalated to another level. She scrounged around the condo, looking for signs that might link Linda and Harry as a couple. Linda had been thorough. She found a small tin can, tore the initial and confidential letters into tiny pieces, lit a match, tossed the pieces inside, and watched them burn. She flushed the ashes down the toilet, flushing several times to get rid of any traces of ash, and placed the tin next to her purse. She surveyed one last time, checking and double-checking for pictures, phone records, or anything, and after finding nothing, she grabbed her purse, tin can, and the letter and went directly to the police.

The events of the past three days had been unbelievable, but the next order of business was finding Linda's mother. She thought nothing worse could happen until finding out Katherine Black had become Katherine Cross and had died in an automobile accident nine months earlier, ironically on the same day Linda was diagnosed with her brain tumor. Her husband, Marvin, had not talked to Linda's sisters since the funeral and was not sure he could locate them. Nevertheless, Tasha gave him the details of the service in hopes he might attend. He informed her he had never met this Linda person and had no reason to come but was quick to ask if a life insurance policy was involved and if Kathy was the beneficiary. Infuriated, Tasha hung up, never responding or saying good-bye.

Chapter 48

Linda's public viewing was held one hour before the funeral. Tasha stood at the head of the coffin, greeting employees and acquaintances, and was surprised by the number of people in attendance. She was not sure if each person knew her or if they were curiosity seekers. She managed to remain cordial even when greeting Dr. Maddox; however, she became weak when seeing a young woman, the spitting image of Linda, approach her.

"Hello," she said, extending her hand. "You must be Natasha Campbell. I am Gail Black, Linda's youngest sister."

Tasha, almost speechless, said, "Yes, I am. It's so… Thank you for coming… I must really sound stupid. I really don't know what to say. Please, please be seated."

"Thank you, but I need to see my sister first."

"Yes… of course. I thought I was seeing Linda when you walked down the aisle. I'm sorry, I was not ready to see someone who looks so much like her. I'm sorry for your loss." Natasha stepped away to allow Gail the chance to spend private time with Linda. She had not seen her in over fifteen years, but this was not the way she pictured their reunion. Gail had not heard from Melissa since their mother's funeral, and the phone number she had was no longer valid. She was surprised Marvin reached out to her but was grateful he had.

Linda's funeral was simple and understated and in total contrast to the life she lived. With Ken, David, and Gail, a total stranger by her side, Tasha felt a sense of comfort for the first time since Linda's death, but her greatest moment was yet to come. At the conclusion of the service, after Linda's coffin had been placed into the hearse and friends were giving their final good-byes, she noticed Dr. Maddox standing off to the side. She saw a genuine sadness on his face. It was as if he did not want to leave. He was staring at the hearse as two uniformed policemen walked up behind him. The expression on his face went from sadness to disbelief and horror. "Dr. Harry James Maddox?" asked one of them.

"Yes," he replied.

"You are under arrest for the murder of Linda Marie Black. You have the right to remain silent. Anything you say can and will be used against you in a court of law. You have the right to an attorney. If you cannot afford an attorney, one will be appointed for you. Do you understand these rights?"

"What... what the hell is this all about? What?" said Harry.

"Do you understand these rights?"

"Yes, but this must be a mistake."

Tasha asked the driver to wait as they watched the police handcuff Harry and place him into the police car. A confused Gail, David, and Ken watched in amazement, but Natasha, with a spirit of justice and relief, smiled as she watched the police vehicle drive away. Natasha thanked the driver for waiting.

Chapter 49

Dr. Harry James Maddox was arraigned for the murder of Linda Marie Black and forced to submit to DNA testing. His world was crumbling before his eyes. He had no idea what was going on and wondered how he could be charged for the murder of the woman he loved.

Katrina was on a mission to find the best legal counsel in Montgomery Valley. Harry was denied bail and spent the night in jail. He was frightened and uncertain about his future for the first time in his life.

The following morning, Harry's lawyer told him things did not look good, saying, "Ms. Black left an incriminating letter implicating you in her death, and the letter was written in her handwriting and signed two days before she died. Semen matching your DNA was found in her vaginal cavity. She died from nitrous oxide poisoning, and your prints were the only set of visible fingerprints on the machine. The fact that her dress was nowhere on the premises nor in her car does not provide a positive spin on the situation or look good for you. The prosecutor will argue that you intentionally discarded or destroyed incriminating evidence. Her DNA was found on the mask used to administer the nitrous oxide. The custodial staff stated that all trash had been removed from the office before they arrived. And, Dr. Maddox, no one is going to believe that she showed up at your office wearing only a trench coat and high heels. The prosecution will argue that you intentionally drove the car to that sleazy motel to get her away from your office and throw suspicion off you. They will also argue that the man who asked the night clerk to call the police fits your physical description. The fact that she had your business card and only your card in her pocket will be viewed as her pointing a finger directly at you, if something was to happen to her. Man, she has you by the fucking nuts."

"Mr. Thomas, none of this makes sense, not even to me. What am I supposed to do?" asked Harry.

"What's your plea?" asked Mr. Thomas.

"I'm innocent… I swear I'm innocent."

"Then we will enter a not-guilty plea. Trust me, this will be a very difficult case. They will dig into anything and every aspect of your life, past and present. They will look for mistresses, hotel receipts, and credit card statements. They will interview every patient, especially female patients, that you have ever treated. It will be difficult, and you're going to have a fight before you. You are going to have to be completely honest with me. Were there other women? Is there anything you have not told me? Did you drive her car to that motel, and was it you that asked the clerk to call the police?"

Harry's heart skipped three beats, and he cautiously answered, "Absolutely not!"

"I'll see you tomorrow. This is your first offense, and you are not considered to be a flight risk, so we should be able to post bail. I am going to fight for your innocence and for your wife and daughters. This will not be easy, but, Dr. Maddox, I pray to God that you are telling me the truth."

"Yes, I'm telling you the truth," Harry said hanging his head in shame.

Harry was reflecting over the night Linda died and said, "That controlling bitch!" She is destroying me even from the grave. She killed herself, and she is taking me with her. She finally screwed me after all. Then he thought about the last words she said to him, "You told me several times you were going to divorce her, but you really had no intention. When you are deep in your grave, know that I love you because I will take this broken love with me to my grave." She had planned her suicide, and she has already taken him to the grave with her. Nothing was left but to bury him. If she could not have him, she made damn sure no one else would. She is controlling his future from the grave, and now he finally understands the wrath of a woman scorned.

Chapter 50

Harry pleaded not guilty to the charge of first-degree murder and was released on bail. The sordid details of Linda's death spread throughout the Valley and beyond. Harry became the laughing stock of the community, and his family was treated as if they were "the plague," and they had done nothing. Katrina barely spoke to him. It was only enough to keep up an appearance of family unity in the community and in front of the girls when they were home.

With the knowledge of her father's arrest, it became difficult for Beverly to remain focused in college, but it helped being hundreds of miles away where she could keep the family secret and embarrassment undercover. However, Angela was not as fortunate. As a junior in high school, the unwavering support of her very best friend Glenda helped her to realize she was not alone. They understood the pain and suffering of their parents and sympathized with both. They sensed their mother's hurt and humiliation, and they were torn between their distrust, love, and hatred for their father. The Cinderella lifestyle they once lived seemed like a fairy tale gone south, and their childhood Prince Charming is now only a figment of their imagination.

The time between Harry's arrest and the trial was fourteen months, which was an eternity for the Maddox household. He could not practice dentistry, and Katrina found a job as a hostess in an upscale restaurant to avoid being in the same house with Harry all day long. Being in the public's eye was the last type of job she wanted, but it was the only place willing to hire her. Angela jumped at the chance to go to summer school and left the Valley immediately after graduation, an event Harry decided not to attend.

Linda's condo was paid off upon her death, and according to her will, it and all contents were left to Natasha Campbell. In addition, there were two life insurance policies in the amount of two hundred and fifty thousand dollars each. One was left to Melissa, and the second policy was left to Gail. Natasha gave the condo and its contents to Gail without asking for anything in return.

During the fourteen months prior to the start of the trial, Natasha brought Gail up to date on Linda's life, and Gail shared everything she could about their lives as children and the effect Linda's leaving had on each of them. Gail and David became great friends appearing to be a better fit for each other than David and Linda. Tasha wondered if this was a true love connection that they had not yet recognized. Although Linda and Gail could have passed for twins, their personalities were completely different. Gail was low-keyed, and her appearance, although striking and beautiful in her own right, was understated compared to Linda.

As predicted, Natasha became the first female vice president of Bethel Industries, LLC, following Mr. O'Malley's retirement. She received an unprecedented salary increase, a corner office on the twenty-seventh floor, and two company vehicles. She certainly earned the position and the accolades to accompany the promotion.

Gail was overjoyed when Natasha asked her to serve as her maid of honor. Gail's creative skills were a welcomed blessing. She hosted a dynamic Parisian-themed bridal shower. The wedding was held in one of the smaller ballrooms at the Montgomery Valley Yacht Club and exemplified the characteristics of Tasha. It was well done, simple and understated, yet elegant. The guest list included only one hundred guests. Natasha was billed as the most beautiful bride of the decade. However, Bethel Industries would not be outdone and claimed exclusive rights to host the reception. The wedding party transitioned into the grand ballroom where every person of nobility within the Bethel family and abroad congregated. The more than five hundred guests dined on lobster, prime rib, oysters, caviar, and escargot, the best that money could buy. And on their behalf, Natasha's private accountant willingly accepted the task of accepting and logging the monetary gifts generously lavished upon them.

Chapter 51

Fourteen months after the death of Linda Marie Black
Six weeks later
The sentencing (September 26)

Natasha Campbell

When Natasha learned the judge was ready to pronounce Harry's sentencing, she immediately returned to the crammed courtroom to find a seat and wait. Her memories of Linda and the trial ran over and over in her head, and she was unable to stop them. It was the most difficult day of her life. She kept secret Linda's willingness as a consenting participant, and now that Harry had been found guilty, she would have to take Linda's confession to her grave. She also had to live with the knowledge that she possibly held the key to reasonable doubt, if not the key to his freedom. Although she was not privy to his side, the one thing she remembered from childhood was that there were always three sides to every story—his, hers, and the truth. Whatever the truth, in the end, he treated Linda as less than human by leaving her in the parking lot of a two-bit hotel.

Natasha's internal and quiet anger demanded revenge, and she wanted Harry James Maddox to rot in hell after spending the rest of his life behind bars. The amount of hatred she possessed toward him was unhealthy and ate at the core of her existence. How many times had he fondled or even penetrated her? What or who in the hell gave him that right? In her head, he was responsible for taking her virginity without permission and killing Linda, and she could never forgive him.

As she waited, she was certain the pounding of her heart could be heard throughout the room and that everyone could see her body vibrating as her heart beat harder and faster. She knew it was going to eventually explode right in front of their eyes. Her body was racked by anxiety as perspiration pasted her blouse to her back. Unable to utter a word or barely breathe, she discreetly took slow deep calming breaths. Ken eventually arrived taking a seat next to her. He reached out and grabbed her wet clammy hand in an attempt to comfort her the only way he knew how, just by being at her side.

Natasha had never met Katrina face to face. She searched the crowd and did not see her. She admired her strength, tenacity, and courage and was empathetic to the woman who had to live through such personal embarrassment and public humiliation.

Tasha felt completely alone. Nothing or no one could fill Linda's void, and it was that single sobering thought that quickly snapped her back into reality. She had to stop the self-pity and remember this trial was not just about her but about all the victims and her promise to Linda as she lay in her coffin. Dr. Harry James Maddox would pay for what he had done. This was the day she lived for… and the day for which Linda died.

Katrina Maddox

Katrina arrived at the courthouse with her sister Roberta, who went inside to be seated. Katrina needed time to gather her thoughts. It would take a person comprised of steel to walk into this courtroom of vultures with their head held high, and she was not that person. She had been stripped of her husband, dignity, and pride. With each witness, a piece of her died with every word uttered. It was as if her spirit was willing but her body was no longer able. Today, she also faced the community of Montgomery Valley.

Nothing could prepare her for this day. She refused to allow the girls to come home, especially wanting to shield them from seeing their father's face when sentenced or being handcuffed and led from the courtroom. Those who once considered them friends wanted nothing more to do with them. Katrina wanted to relocate but was determined to see Harry through to the end despite the humiliation. The discomfort the trial caused to their family was the very thing that brought her and the girls closer together, providing an unbreakable source of strength. They were Harry's most vulnerable victims further scrutinized by a sanctimonious community.

Today would mark a new beginning. Montgomery Valley could put this ordeal behind them. Harry would know the fate of his future, and Katrina would tell him she was filing for divorce and relocating to a place where she would no longer walk in shame.

As time drew closer to Harry's arrival, Katrina's stomach began to churn. She felt weak. Her bladder played tricks, sending her to the bathroom three times in thirty minutes. Suddenly she heard someone call her name. "Mrs. Maddox, would you like to come into the courtroom? Your husband is on his way in."

Katrina bent over in excruciating pain when a sharp sting tore through her gut. She attempted to straighten up, but it was impossible. A second pain immediately ripped through her as she lost her balance, and the bailiff broke her fall. "Please sit down," he said. She knew time was running out and shook her head negatively. With his help, but still unable to speak, she forced herself to place one foot in front of the other, slowly maneuvering her way inside. She sat down in the rear of the room, far from the seat reserved for her, grasping Roberta's hand.

Vincent Landry

When Vincent heard of the news of Dr. Harry James Maddox, his life changed, becoming surreal. After reality and the truth set in and his world stopped spinning, he felt Harry did not deserve to live. He knew the law well enough to know he could be a free man within the blink of an eye. Vincent was wired to believe in the judicial system, but in this case, the law failed everyone, especially Paris who would never be stable enough to testify on her own behalf.

His presence had been noticeable throughout the trial, never missing a day. He sat in the same seat, rocking back and forth, back and forth, his rhythm never changing. His facial expression was indecipherable. He was a ticking time bomb, becoming uncharacteristically cold and calculated and building an impenetrable fortress around himself. He acknowledged no one, not even his brethren in the judicial system. His piercing glare remained fixed upon Harry regardless of the person on the witness stand. He clung to every movement Harry made. Those who knew him were concerned with his change in behavior, but those who really knew him sympathized with him, a man with one cheating wife and another who was mentally unbalanced. And he felt no need to explain his actions. The last four months had taken its toll on his nervous system.

Vincent was crushed that the charge of first-degree murder could not be supported.

Linda's letter was compelling but not strong enough to prove that Harry planned to kill her. California's death penalty was declared unconstitutional, and the state had not executed a prisoner since 2006. In California, involuntary manslaughter occurs when one person kills another unintentionally, either (1) while committing a crime that is not an inherently dangerous California felony or (2) while committing a lawful act that might produce death without due caution. However, in his eyes, Linda's death was intentional.

Today was difficult. He was suffocating on the very air that kept him alive. The anxiety and waiting chilled him through to the bone. He was determined not to leave the courtroom until he came face to face with Harry. He had not figured out how but that he would.

Chapter 52

Harry felt isolated being behind bars for six weeks without visitors other than his attorney. He felt abandoned by Katrina and was not strong enough to face his daughters. He had a lot of time to do nothing but think. He fell back in love with Katrina for proving to be the wife he needed from the beginning. He hated Linda for becoming the manipulative, jealous, fatal attraction that would rather see him dead than to be without him. He was angry with the eight patients for lying on the witness stand, making him seem like a sex-crazed monster. He felt victimized, hating everyone for what they had done to him. There was no doubt in his mind that he was going to prison and was afraid he might not be tough enough to endure it. He was not street-tested and thoughts of suicide had been on his mind. He was monitored closely because he was not going to rob the Valley of their moment. He had come to the conclusion that the cards were stacked against him from the beginning, and if he could, he would actually kill Linda right now. He was angry that he was willing to give up everything for her, and by her orchestration, he had.

Thinking about the testimonies of those who lied made his stomach curdle. He would not touch most of them even with a paper sack over their head. The fact that none of the women could remember what happened was the exact intent of the nitrous oxide. There were only three women—one was dead, one was in a mental hospital, and the other was sitting in the courtroom in silence. Did she really know what happened?

He dodged many bullets during the trial. The motel night clerk could not say, without a doubt, that Harry was the man who came into the lobby and asked that the police be called. There was no evidence connecting him as the driver or passenger in Linda's car. He had used rubber gloves and surgical wear over his shoes and removed everything, stuffing it into his pocket upon exiting. After leaving the lobby, he walked several blocks to a bus stop. He then rode the bus for approximately three and a half miles before getting off and walking the rest of the way back to his office. He opened the trunk of his car and emptied the contents of his pockets in the trash taken from the office. He strategically wrapped each earring and the necklace separately, hoping if one piece were found, someone would think it was simply a lost piece of jewelry. He drove to a highly populated area loaded with highly frequented restaurants, parked his car near the entrance, put on his fedora, pulled his collar up around his neck, and walked down the alley, throwing the evidence into four different dumpsters in hopes it would be mixed among the garbage and never be found, and it was not.

Harry was led into the courtroom in view of the many angry and judgmental faces he referred to as gawkers, many he had never seen before. However, there were four faces he saw regularly, Katrina, Gail, Natasha, and the man with the possessed and piercing eyes. He searched the room for Katrina, desperately needing her support. She was not seated in the seat normally reserved for her. He looked into Natasha's eyes and saw a smirk on her face, one he had never seen before. Instinctively his gut told him Natasha knew everything. Gail was seated to her right, and each time the sight of her made him feel like he was seeing Linda's ghost. Ken was on her left. He needed Gail to know that he was sorry and he loved Linda and did not kill her. Gail only wanted her sister's death avenged. The man with the piercing eyes was characteristically rocking back and forth, back and forth, as he had done since the beginning of the trial, and his frightening expression never changed. Harry continued to span the room in search of Katrina, only seeing Roberta, who refused to look at him. Harry lowered his head in shame. It was over and Linda had won.

"All rise" was all Harry heard before zoning out. "Harry James Maddox, you have been found guilty, by a jury of your peers, of involuntary manslaughter in the death of Linda Marie Black. In my opinion, justice has not been served. An outstanding woman of the community has died because of your negligence. Eight women have been raped and their reputations damaged because you used poor judgment. This has been one of the most heinous misuses of power I have ever encountered in my career as a judge. You have taken an honorable profession and turned it into a circus. You have violated the trust of the public and have put a cloud of mistrust over the heads of every honest and respectable dentist. You are despicable and a disgrace to man. I wish I could sentence you to death, but law states otherwise. I wished it didn't. This is where I disagree with the law, but I am bound by an oath to uphold the laws of the state of California. Involuntary manslaughter carries a prison sentence of up to four years in a federal prison."

The gasp of the crowd was one of disbelief. "Silence, please... Therefore I will assert my judicial powers to ensure that nothing like this will ever happen again... at least not by you! On count one, on the charge of involuntary manslaughter, you will serve four years in the state penitentiary. On counts four through eleven, of eight counts of rape under Penal Code 261(a)(3) and (4), where each count carries a sentence of up to six years and a fine of seventy thousand dollars, you will serve the maximum sentence of six years for each count. It is the decision of this court that each count is served consecutively; therefore, you should not see the light of day for fifty-two years. A fine will not be imposed because your family is as much of a victim as the people of this fine city, and I pray that one day they will find it in their hearts to forgive you and be able to move forward with their lives. You and your attorney have the right to appeal." The judge looked over his reading glasses with a look of disgust and asked, "Do you have anything to say to the victims or the families of the victims?"

"Yes, Your Honor... I do," said Harry. He turned to face the crowd. "I want to apologize to the residents of Montgomery Valley. I ask you to forgive me for my indiscretions. I am not the monster I have been portrayed to be. I have not touched the women who have testified. I know you don't believe me." The crowd heckled him. The judge demanded order in the court. "Thank you, Your Honor." Harry continued with a tone of sincerity in his voice. "I do ask for forgiveness and ask that you not hold my wife or my children responsible for anything I may have done." He finally saw Katrina in the rear of the courthouse, this time his eyes meeting hers. "I'm so sorry, Katrina, for what I have put you and the girls through. I'm so sorry. I am not the monster these women have portrayed me to be. I have not touched any of them. I swear to God that I have not touched these women, that I promise. I swear on my father's grave. I know that I decided not to take the stand on my behalf, not because I was hiding what I may or may not have done, according to the court, but because I knew that I had been tried and convicted before the trial began. I knew the evidence was stacked against me, and after listening to the testimony of so many women, I did not stand a chance, and that is the only reason. I have made some bad choices, and I own that, but I want you all to know that none of you, not you or you or you did I touch, rest well knowing that. Not one woman who took the stand told the truth. Not one... I made a mistake, and I did fall in love with Linda. An embarrassed Katrina dropped her head. Yes, I fell in love. I loved you, Katrina, and I will always love you. I didn't think it was possible, but I loved both of you, and I could not make a decision, but that did not make me a murderer. I did not kill her, and we were in love with each other. I don't know why Linda did what she did; she must have turned up the controls. I swear to God I did not. Yes, I led her to believe I was going to divorce Katrina. I'm sorry, Katrina. I guess I didn't know how to walk away because I needed her in my life. Katrina, tell the girls I love them and that I am truly sorry. I am so very sorry for the shame and embarrassment I brought to our family and to the people of Montgomery Valley. You accepted me as a member of this community, and we loved it here. I beg your forgiveness, but to those who testified, your reputation is still intact, your bodies are still pure. You were never touched. You were never touched by me and that each of you can take to the bank!" he said as the tears welled up in his eyes, and he began crying.

Then the judge asked if any of the women who testified had anything to say. The man with the piercing eyes stood up and said, "I do, Your Honor."

A confused Judge Patterson looked at him and said, "Yes, Attorney Landry, this is a bit unusual. What would you like to say? Is it related to this trial?"

The moment Harry heard him addressed as Attorney Landry, he knew immediately who he was. He sensed the shit was getting ready to hit the fan but had no more fight left.

"May I come forward, Your Honor? I would like to face the accused."

"Yes, please, the courtroom is yours. Please come forward."

Vincent walked up to Harry and looked him directly in the eyes. Vincent stepped into him as Harry stepped back. "I want to share something with you. My wife is Paris. I loved her, adored her. She was my life. She was beautiful and fun-loving. She made me believe again, laugh again, hope again, and feel like I had a reason for living. You do remember my wife, don't you?" Harry dropped his eyes, remaining silent as his Adam's apple moved up and down in his throat. The bombshell of all bombshells was getting ready to hit the fan, and Harry could only hope he could handle the blow. "Look at me… look at me!" shouted Vincent. "Paris was my wife, my second wife. My first wife cheated on me, not once, not twice, but after three or four times. I quit counting. I promised myself I would never marry again. Then one day I met the most beautiful woman I had ever seen. She was my angel. She was different, and she was good, had a beautiful heart, everything an old man like me could want. I couldn't believe she wanted me, and it was equally hard to believe she could love me, but she did. I had a vasectomy after my first divorce because I did not want to bring more children into such an evil world. But for our third anniversary, I had the procedure reversed because she deserved a child. We tried and tried to conceive. We had several unsuccessful in vitro fertilization attempts, but one day she came home excited and told me she was pregnant. I could not believe it because the doctors kept telling me my sperm count was low. Finally, they convinced me that the baby was mine. They said if I did not have a reason to believe she was unfaithful, then I was the father. She was the committed wife, she was my life." The courtroom became silent, and one could hear a pin drop. No one wanted to miss what might come next. "Then one day her water broke. We were so happy. Our baby was coming. We were planning to name our son Jacques. He was born. I was there, and my wife delivered a beautiful healthy *black* baby boy." The court was so quiet one could hear a church house mouse run through it. "I told the world my baby died, but in truth, my baby was never born." The courtroom erupted into shouts of disbelief.

"Order in the court, order in the court!" screamed Judge Patterson. "If you cannot control yourselves, I will have the bailiff clear the courtroom."

Harry was stunned and speechless, because he, like everyone else, believed the baby died.

"Let me finish. My wife, Paris, was so confused. I accused her of being unfaithful. I called her every single inappropriate name in the book. But she never knew! She never knew! You bastard, you sick son of a bitch!"

"Attorney Landry, watch your mouth. This is still a court of law. Are you finished?" asked Judge Patterson.

"Almost, Your Honor… Almost. I do apologize. My wife had a nervous breakdown. To this day, she is still asking about her baby, the white one… and not the black one she actually gave birth to. You ruined our lives… all of our lives. Yes, I kept it out of the news that the baby she gave birth to was black. I was ashamed and did not want the world to know that my wife, my beautiful and young wife, Paris, was just as manipulative and unfaithful as my first wife, only this was worse. She became impregnated by a black man. I was ashamed of her, and now I am so damn ashamed of myself. I am so sorry for the way I treated her. Not anymore. Let me show you something." As he leaned closer into Harry, the bailiff attempted to hold it him back.

"It's all right," said the judge. "He is one of us. He knows just how far he can go."

"I want to show you something. When this trial began, I knew immediately that she never knew. She trusted you. I am a man of means, and I had the baby's DNA tested. I want to show you a picture… a picture of your son. Do you want to see it?" He reached into his pocket and pulled out the picture of a beautiful young child and put it in his face. "Do you see him? Do you see him? I want you to take the image of your son to hell with you!" he said screaming.

The court erupted into noise and confusion, and the last thing Harry felt was a sharp instrument piercing his chest straight through his heart.

About the Author

Brooklynn Nicole lived a sheltered childhood with just enough freedom to be exposed to the hard realities of life. Her writing is a compilation of her vivid imagination and life experiences. As a child, she was a loner, shy, talked about, and even bullied, so she buried herself behind a pencil and a pad of paper. She did not write because she felt she was a prolific writer; she just wanted to express her feeling when there was no one else she trusted to understand exactly how she felt. Growing up was difficult, wishing daily she had a sister to whom she could express herself. As an adult, she is thankful for the life she lives, the experiences that shaped her into the woman she has become, and the friend who became the sister she never had. She is equally grateful for the love and gift of writing and accepts this opportunity as a challenge to fully express herself. She loves fiction because it encourages her to expound upon her creativity and take liberties with the realities of her imagination. She challenges every reader to discern truth from fiction and to identify with one's personal truth by learning and growing from it. Step up and step out with the wisdom and courage to overcome obstacles that will forever attempt to pull you into a downward spiral.